Maya Blake's hopes ... when she picked up l ... did she know her dre ... still pinch herself every now and then to make sure it's not a dream? Yes, she does! Feel free to pinch her, too, via Twitter, Facebook or Goodreads! Happy reading!

Books by Maya Blake

Mills & Boon Modern Romance

Signed Over to Santino
A Diamond Deal with the Greek
Married for the Prince's Convenience
Innocent in His Diamonds

Rival Brothers

A Deal with Alejandro
One Night with Gael

The Billionaire's Legacy

The Di Sione Secret Baby

Secret Heirs of Billionaires

Brunetti's Secret Son

Seven Sexy Sins

A Marriage Fit for a Sinner

The Untameable Greeks

What the Greek's Money Can't Buy
What the Greek Can't Resist
What the Greek Wants Most

Visit the Author Profile page
at millsandboon.co.uk for more titles.

To Carly, for making my stories shine!

PROLOGUE

NOTHING HAD CHANGED in six years.

Emiliano Castillo was mildly surprised at himself for entertaining the thought, even for a second, that things would be different. Wasn't 'the old way or no way' one of the endless tenets forming his family's foundations and beliefs?

Wasn't that rigid clinging to tradition one of *his* reasons for turning his back on his family?

He kept his gaze dead straight, refusing to turn his head to glance at the miles of rolling paddocks that usually held his family's prized thoroughbreds and foal training ground. Even then, he couldn't help but notice, as his chauffeur drove him towards his ancestral home, that the normally teeming landscape was now curiously empty, the dozen or so gauchos usually in each corral nowhere in sight.

He brought his wandering thoughts back under control. There would be no indulging in nostalgia on this visit. In fact, Emiliano intended the trip to the renowned Castillo Estate just outside Cordoba, Argentina, to be as brief as the summons that had brought him here.

He had only come out of respect for Matias, his older brother. Had Matias been in a position to speak, Emiliano would've made sure his brother relayed his refusal of the summons he'd received in London loud and clear to their parents.

Sadly, Matias wasn't in a position to do any such thing.

The reason for that tightened his jaw, even as a brief tinge of sadness assailed him. Thankfully, there was little time to dwell on it as the car drew up in front of the extensive luxury villa in which several generations of proud, intractable Castillos had lived.

Oak double doors opened as he stepped out of the car.

Emiliano tensed, for a moment forgetting that neither his father nor his mother had deigned to open doors of their own accord for as long as he could remember. Not when they had servants to do it for them.

Mounting the steps, he nodded curtly at the ageing butler's greeting. This particular member of staff wasn't one he remembered and for that he was marginally thankful. He wanted no more memories triggered, or to go down the lonely, dismal path he'd done his best to try to forget.

'If señor would like to come with me, Señor and Señora Castillo are waiting in the drawing room.'

Emiliano allowed himself the briefest of glances at the walls that surrounded the home he'd grown up in, the sturdy bannister he used to slide down as a child, the antique cabinet he'd crashed into and earned himself a long-since-healed fracture on his collarbone.

He'd had time to do all that because he hadn't been the firstborn son. His time had been his own to use or misuse as he pleased, because only one person had counted in this household: Matias. But it was only as he'd entered his teenage years that he'd grown to fathom exactly what that meant.

Securing the button on his single-breasted suit, he refocused his gaze and followed the butler into the wide, sunlit reception room.

His parents were seated in twin wing-backed chairs that wouldn't have been out of place in the throne room at the Palace of Versailles. But, even without the heavy accoutrements and almost-garish displays of wealth to punctuate their success, Benito and Valentina Castillo carried themselves with near-royal pride.

They both eyed him now with equal expressions of hauteur and indifference—both expressions he was used to. But Emiliano glimpsed something else beneath the brittle exteriors.

Nerves. Desperation.

He tucked that observation away, walked forward and kissed his mother on both cheeks.

'Mama, I hope you are well?'

Her expression twitched only for as long as it took for her to give him a once-over, before settling back into prideful superiority. 'Of course. But I would be better still if you'd bothered to answer us when we first reached out to you. But, as usual, you choose to do things in your own time, when it suits you best.'

Emiliano gritted his teeth and curbed the urge to remind them that it was the legacy of forgetful indifference they'd bestowed on him which had dictated his actions. Instead he nodded to his father, received a curt nod in return and selected an armchair to settle in.

'I am here now. Shall we get on with why you summoned me?' he said, then refused the offer of a drink from the butler.

His father's mouth twisted. '*Sí*, always in a rush. Always, you have somewhere else to be, don't you?'

Emiliano slowly exhaled. 'As a matter of fact, I do.' He was in the middle of a bidding war for a revolutionary social media programme back in London. The programme's creators were being courted by at least half a dozen other venture capitalists. Despite his company being the biggest and most powerful of them all, he reminded himself that he'd been the underdog once, before a daring move had set him on his way to stratospheric success. This wasn't a time to take his foot off the pedal.

He also had to approve the finishing touches for the birthday celebration his event planner had put together for Sienna Newman.

His vice-president of Acquisitions.

His lover.

Thoughts of the woman whose intellect kept him on his toes by day and whose body thrilled his by night fractionally allayed the bitter memories of his childhood. Unlike his past liaisons, she hadn't been an easy conquest, her reluctance even to give him the time of day beyond the boardroom was a challenge that had fired his blood in the months before she'd even agreed to have dinner with him.

In his quiet moments, Emiliano still silently reeled at the changes he'd made in his life in order to accommodate his lover. The few who presumed to know him would agree— rightly, in this instance—that this behaviour wasn't like him at all. His own disquiet in the face of the reservation he sometimes felt from Sienna made him question himself. But not enough to disrupt the status quo. Not yet, anyway. Although, like everything in life, it, too, had a finite shelf life. It was that ticking clock which made him even more impatient to be done with whatever this summons was all about and get out of this place.

He stared at his parents with a raised eyebrow, letting the silent censure bounce off him. He'd long ago learned that nothing he said or did would ever change their attitude towards him. He was the spare they'd sired but never needed. His place would be on a shelf, fed, clothed, but collecting dust and nothing else. So he'd left home and stopped trying.

'When was the last time you visited your brother?' his mother enquired, her fixed expression breaking momentarily to allow a touch of humanity to filter through at the mention of Matias.

The question brought to mind his brother's current state. Comatose in a hospital bed in Switzerland with worryingly low signs of brain activity.

Emiliano weathered the punch of sadness and brushed

a speck of lint off his cuff. 'Two weeks ago. And every two weeks before that since his accident four months ago,' he replied.

His parents exchanged surprised glances. He curbed the urge to laugh. 'If this is all you needed to know, you could've sent me an email.'

'It isn't. But we find it…reassuring that family still means something to you, seeing as you abandoned it without a backward glance,' Benito stated.

The fine hairs on Emiliano's nape lifted. 'Reassuring? I guess it should be celebrated that I've done something right at last, then? But, at the risk of straying into falsehoods and hyperbole, perhaps let's stick to the subject of why you asked me here.'

Benito picked up his glass and stared into the contents for a few seconds before he knocked it back and swallowed with a gulp. The action was so alien—his father's outward poise a thing so ingrained it seemed part of his genetic make-up—that Emiliano's jaw threatened to drop before he caught himself.

Setting the glass down with a brisk snap, another first, Benito eyed him with fresh censure. Nothing new there.

'We're broke. Completely destitute. Up the proverbial creek without a paddle.'

'Excuse me?' Emiliano wasn't sure whether it was the bald language that alarmed him or his father's continued acting out of character.

'You wish me to repeat myself? Why? So you can gloat?' his father snapped. 'Very well. The polo business, the horse breeding. Everything has failed. The estate has been sliding into the red for the past three years, ever since Rodrigo Cabrera started his competing outfit here in Cordoba. We approached Cabrera and he bought the debt. Now he's calling in the loans. If we don't pay up by the end of next month, we will be thrown out of our home.'

Emiliano realised his jaw was clenched so tight he had to force it apart to speak. 'How can that be? Cabrera doesn't know the first thing about horse breeding. The last I heard he was dabbling in real estate. Besides, Castillo is the foremost polo-training and horse-breeding establishment in South America. How can you be on the brink of bankruptcy?' he demanded.

His mother's colour receded and her fingers twisted the white lace handkerchief in her hand. 'Watch your tone, young man.'

Emiliano inhaled sharply, stopped the sharper words that threatened to spill and chose his words carefully. 'Explain to me how these circumstances have occurred.'

His father shrugged. 'You are a man of business…you know how these things go. A few bad investments here and there…'

Emiliano shook his head. 'Matias was…*is*…a shrewd businessman. He would never have let things slide to the point of bankruptcy without mitigating the losses or finding a way to reverse the business's fortunes. At the very least, he would've told me…' He stopped when his parents exchanged another glance. 'I think you should tell me what's really going on. I'm assuming you asked me here because you need my help?'

Pride flared in his father's eyes for a blinding moment before he glanced away and nodded. '*Sí.*' The word was one Emiliano was sure he didn't want to utter.

'Then let's have it.'

They remained stoically silent for several heartbeats before his father rose. He strode to a cabinet on the far side of the room, poured himself another drink and returned to his chair. Setting the glass down, he picked up a tablet Emiliano hadn't spotted before and activated it.

'Your brother left a message for you. Perhaps it would explain things better.'

He frowned. 'A message? How? Matias is in a coma.'

Valentina's lips compressed, distress marring her features for a brief second. 'You don't need to remind us. He recorded it before his brain operation, once the doctors gave him the possible prognosis.'

Emiliano couldn't fault the pain in her voice or the sadness in her eyes. And, not for the first time in his life, he wondered why that depth of feeling for his brother had never spilt over for him.

Pushing the fruitless thought aside, he focused on the present. On what he could control.

'That was two months ago. Why are you only telling me about this message now?'

'We didn't think it would be needed before now.'

'And by *it*, you mean me?'

His mother shrugged. Knowing the iron control he'd locked down on his feelings where his parents were concerned was in danger of breaking free and exploding, he jerked to his feet. Crossing the room to his father, he held out his hand for the tablet.

Benito handed it over.

Seeing his brother's face frozen on the screen, the bandage around his head and the stark hospital furniture and machines around him, Emiliano felt his breath strangle in his chest. Matias was the one person who hadn't dismissed him for being born second. His brother's support was the primary reason Emiliano had broken away from the glaringly apathetic environment into which he'd been born. He knew deep down that he would've made it, no matter what, but Matias's unwavering encouragement had bolstered him in the early, daunting years when he'd been floundering alone on the other side of the world.

He stemmed the tremor moving through him as his gaze moved over his brother's pale, gaunt face. Returning to his seat, he pressed the play button.

The message was ten minutes long.

With each second of footage that passed, with each word his brother uttered, Emiliano sank further into shock and disbelief. When it was over, he lifted his gaze and met equal stares that were now less indifferent and more... concerned.

'Are you... Is this for real?' he demanded.

'You're hearing the words from your brother's lips and still you doubt it?' his father asked, a trace of shame lacing his stiff demeanour.

'I don't doubt what Matias is saying. I'm questioning whether you truly gambled away millions that you knew the company couldn't afford!'

His father slammed his hand on the table. 'Castillo is my company!'

'It's also Matias's birthright! At least, that's what you drummed into him from the day he was born, was it not? Wasn't that the reason he all but broke his back to make it a success? Because you pressured him to succeed at all costs?'

'I am no tyrant. What he did for Castillo, he did willingly.'

Emiliano barely managed to bite back the swear word that hovered on his tongue. 'And for that you repay him by frittering away the profits behind his back?'

'The deal we made with Cabrera was supposed to be a sure thing.'

'A sure thing? You were duped by a man who spotted an easy score a mile away.' He stared down at the screen, still unable to believe the tale Matias had told. Bankruptcy. Destitution for his parents. Absurd promises made. Regret that the burden now fell on Emiliano's shoulders.

The naked plea in his brother's eyes and solemn tone not to let the family down.

That last entreaty, more than anything else, was what

kept Emiliano from walking out the door in that moment. Even though what Matias was asking of him—the request to honour the deal his parents had struck with Rodrigo Cabrera—was so ludicrous, he wondered why he wasn't laughing his head off.

Because every single word was true. He could tell just from looking into his parents' eyes.

'You really are serious, aren't you? You struck this bargain that Matias would marry Cabrera's daughter if the deal went south and the loans became due?' he rasped with renewed disbelief. 'Isn't she still a child?'

A brief memory of a little girl in pigtails chasing around the ranch during family visits flitted through his mind. Matias, as usual, had been patient and caring with Graciela Cabrera, but Emiliano, fully immersed in dreams of escape, could barely remember her, save for a few exchanges at the dinner table.

'She's twenty-three years old,' his mother supplied. 'She may have had a few wild escapades that have left her parents with more grey hairs than they wish, but she is more mature now. Matias was her favourite, of course, but she remembers you fondly—'

'I don't care how she remembers me. What I care about is that none of this set-up rang any alarm bells for you!' He seethed, unwilling to rise to the subtle dig. 'From a supposed family friend!'

For the first time, his father had the grace to look embarrassed. But the expression didn't last long. He regrouped, as was the Castillo way. 'We are where we are, Emiliano. The burden of our family's fortunes now rests with you. And don't bother taking out your chequebook. Cabrera has made it clear he wants only one thing. You either marry Graciela Cabrera or you can sit back and watch your mother and me lose everything.'

CHAPTER ONE

SIENNA NEWMAN STEPPED out of the shower, finished drying off and eased her black hair from the tight bun it'd been in all day. Swiping her hand across the steamed-up vanity mirror, she couldn't resist smiling at herself.

Sister Margaret from the orphanage where Sienna had spent most of her childhood had often told her to count her blessings. Of course, counting those blessings while smiling goofily at herself in the mirror would've been met with a frown. The orphanage matriarch certainly wouldn't have approved of the illicitly carnal thrill that went through her as she smoothed expensive and luxurious lotion over her skin, her senses revving up in anticipation of what the evening ahead held for her. It was a good thing therefore that Sister M, as the children had referred to her, wasn't here to see this tiny fall from grace. Because, even with the old biddy's beady eyes on her, Sienna didn't think she could've stopped smiling.

Today, her twenty-eighth birthday had started in spectacular style. Four giant bouquets of calla lilies and white roses, her favourite flowers, had been delivered to her desk on the hour between nine o'clock and midday, each time with a jaw-dropping present wrapped in white silk paper and black velvet bows. The stunning beauty of the diamond tennis bracelet delivered at eleven o'clock had only been topped by the magnificent sapphire teardrop necklace with matching earrings at midday. But even more special than all the presents had been the handwritten notes from Emiliano accompanying each gift. The scrawls had been as bold and domineering as the man, nowhere near flowery, but the intimate words of desire and felicitation had touched her deeply.

The afternoon had taken a different but nevertheless incredible turn, with culinary delights from edible-gold-dusted chocolate to caviar to a single pink-and-silver frosted cupcake with a lit candle for her to wish on and blow out.

She'd made a wish all right. One that had stealthily sprung into her heart and taken root about three months ago, around the time it had dawned on her that she'd been in a relationship with a hitherto unattainable man for almost a year.

Extreme self-preservation born of painful past experiences had fuelled her need to ignore the growing wish, but with each day that passed she'd began to hope rejection wasn't on the cards for her this time, as it had so often been.

As Sienna re-entered the bedroom, her smile dimmed a touch.

The only slight downside to her fantastic day had been the need to once more be evasive in the face of interest from colleagues about her love life and the knowledge that, although his extravagant birthday surprises had been thrilling to experience, Emiliano had once again run roughshod over her need to keep their relationship private.

The last time she'd touched on the subject, they'd rowed, Emiliano's Latin temper erupting in a torrent that had included his adamant refusal to 'skulk around in shadows' or 'pretend I'm not into you when we're in public.'

After a heated back-and-forth on the subject they'd retreated to the not-so-neutral zone of their bedroom, where he'd expressed his extreme displeasure passionately.

Sienna blushed in recollection, but her smile remained elusive, her heart skidding again as a different issue interrupted her happiness.

Another thing that would've made her birthday perfect was Emiliano's presence. Or, barring that, a simple phone call.

All she'd received was an email wishing her happy birthday and a single line to say he was aboard his plane, flying back home from Argentina. Although she'd been relieved that the unexpected extension of his overseas trip by four more days was finally over, she'd yearned to hear his voice. So much so, she'd called him straight back the moment she'd got home, only to have her call go to voicemail. Same as most of her calls the last three days. The one time he'd picked up, he'd been brusque to the point of monosyllabic.

She curbed the tiny spurt of anxiety and pulled on her underwear before sliding on the dress she'd shopped for for hours before discovering it in a tiny shop in Soho. The blood-red sleeveless gown showed off the slight tan she'd gained from their recent weekend away in St Tropez. Fastening her new necklace and earrings, she brushed out her shoulder-length black hair and stepped into black stilettos. The added height would be nowhere near Emiliano's six-foot-three-inch frame, but the confidence boost was nevertheless welcome.

Exhaling, she pushed away the insidious voice that wouldn't remain silent, reminding her that everything in her life—bar her career—thus far, had been ripped from her. That what she had with Emiliano would follow suit. After adding the finishing touches of perfume, clutch and wrap, she headed for the door.

She didn't want to, but Sienna couldn't stop the nerves that assailed her, or the equal amounts of excitement and dread that fluttered through her stomach at the notion of going out in public with Emiliano tonight. Even though they'd never resolved their argument, he'd grown increasingly possessive of her in public recently, his bold caresses almost baiting her to protest. Unwilling to provoke another disagreement, she hadn't, and in her quiet moments even admitted to enjoying those displays. Nevertheless, the butterflies in her stomach grew, their wings beating so loud she almost missed her phone buzzing with a text message.

Her heart skipped a beat when she saw Emiliano's name on her screen.

Slight change of plan. We'll dine at home. Restaurant delivery is taken care of. Let me know if that suits? E.

Her smile burst forth anew, her heart squeezing with happiness as she quickly answered.

That more than suits. Can't wait to see you! XXX

Hitting Send, she stared at the little faint bubble that said her message was being read. Then waited. He didn't answer.

Swallowing, she returned her phone to the clutch and left the bedroom.

The restaurant they were supposed to dine at was a mere two miles away from the Knightsbridge penthouse she shared with Emiliano. And, if Emiliano had already contacted her favourite chef, then the meal was most likely already on its way.

She walked down the stunningly decorated hallway and through the vast sitting room to find Alfie, their young live-in butler, setting the table in the dining room.

He looked up and smiled when he saw her. 'Good evening, miss.'

She returned his smile and nodded at the table. 'Looks like Emiliano has given you the heads-up on the change of plan?'

'Indeed. He's also given me the night off,' he replied

with a grin. 'I'll just wait for the delivery to arrive then I'll leave you two alone to enjoy your birthday.'

She fought the blush that threatened, recalling the butler's wry comment months ago about how he'd become the grateful recipient of many sudden nights off since she'd moved in with Emiliano. 'Thanks.'

Alfie nodded and went back to laying the table. Not wishing to intrude, she drifted back into the living room. Decorated with luxury and deep comfort in mind, the slate-coloured sofas, matching tables and the white walls were interspersed with dark-gold throw pillows and rugs that added welcoming warmth to the large room. A dominating fireplace was aglow to complement the November autumnal weather.

Sienna strolled to the mantel, picked up the single picture adorning it and stared down at the selfie she'd taken of herself and Emiliano three months ago. It had been a rare moment of throwing caution to the wind and all the more special for it. On a late-afternoon stroll in the park across from the penthouse, after a morning and afternoon spent making love, she'd confessed to sadness at not having photographic mementos of a childhood spent in foster care, no matter how wretched. Emiliano had insisted she seize the moment to make a memory. And, even though he'd refused to look into the camera, his years of avoiding the glare of the paparazzi's lens deeply ingrained, he'd posed for the picture. The end result was Emiliano staring at her while she looked into the camera, flushed and self-conscious from his brazenly hungry scrutiny.

He'd taken a look at the photo, pronounced himself satisfied and promptly printed and framed it for the mantel.

Sienna stared at the profile of the man who commanded her days and nights, the boss who'd changed his own company's rules, despite her many blithely ignored protests, in order to date her. Her heart skipped another beat, and with it the secret wish lurking in her heart.

Emiliano Castillo had done more than amend his company's rules. He'd gone on to trigger a few more firsts, as she'd found out in the months following the start of their relationship. For a start, he hadn't been one for *relationships*. Certainly not one with a vice-president of his venture capitalist firm. Most of his liaisons only lasted a couple of months. He'd also never lived with a lover. And he'd certainly never lived with one for going on six months!

Which was why Sienna was daring to believe that theirs was more than a supercharged physical affair. It was why she'd found herself hoping for more. They had never talked about a family, largely because the subject had been strictly off-limits for both of them, save for unavoidable instances that filtered through their lives.

As far as she knew, his relationship with his parents was strained at best, but she'd seen his devastation when his brother had been seriously injured in a car accident four months ago. And, with each trip she'd accompanied him on to the state-of-the-art medical facility in Switzerland where Matias was being cared for after his brain surgery had left him in a coma, she'd witnessed Emiliano's distress and sadness.

Hers was a different story. She had no past to discuss, so she never did.

The desolation she'd learned to live with overpowered her for a single moment before she pushed it back into its designated box. Today was her birthday. She was lucky she had a date to celebrate. But she'd also worked hard to make a life for herself, and she was determined it wouldn't fall victim to rejection and heartache.

So celebrate she *would*.

She returned the picture to the mantel in time to hear the penthouse door's electronic lock disengage.

Expecting it to be Alfie, taking delivery of their food, her heart leapt into her throat when Emiliano walked in.

He was supposed to have been gone for two days. He'd been gone for six. She hadn't comprehended just how much she'd missed him until he handed over the food boxes to Alfie and walked tall and proud into the living room. A rush of longing and happiness overtook her as her gaze met his.

At six foot three, with a powerful but streamlined physique, Emiliano Castillo gave the term 'tall, dark and handsome' full, visceral meaning. But he also carried an extra edge that ensured that heads, and hearts, turned whenever he graced humanity with his presence. His wasn't a flawless face, to start with. A scar sustained along his right jawline from a horse-riding accident as a teenager evoked a sense of illicit danger, if you just looked at him. Bold slants of jet eyebrows over brooding, dark, coppery eyes and a full and sensual mouth sculpted for long, steamy lovemaking nights made him very difficult to look away from.

So she stared, transfixed, heart slamming against her ribs, as he walked slowly towards her. He stopped several feet from where she stood. Electricity crackled through the air as they stared at one another. Then slowly, his eyes traced her body from head to toe, lingering, *possessing*, and back again.

Expecting him to stride forward and sweep her into his arms in that overwhelmingly possessive and blatantly male way he employed, she braced herself, her every sense leaping with excitement.

But he remained where he stood.

'Happy birthday, *querida*. You look exquisite.' His voice was deep, laced with the Spanish intonation he carried proudly. But the words, despite being felicitous and complimentary, were a touch grave. As were the hands he shoved deep into his pockets instead of using them to reach for her as he normally did when they'd been apart this long.

Her heart skittered, but Sienna pushed away the fizzle of anxiety. 'Thank you. It's great to have you back,' she replied, with her tongue lightly slicking lips gone nervous and dry.

His eyelids descended for a moment, then his head tilted slightly, dark eyes resting on her, seeming to absorb her every expression. 'Have you had a good day?' he asked.

The reminder of how her day had gone brought a smile. His breath seemed to catch as her smile widened. 'It was wonderful, Emiliano. I'm not sure how you planned everything without my knowledge but I loved every second of it. Thank you so much for these...' She caressed her necklace and earrings. 'I should be angry with you for forcing me to field questions, though.' She deliberately infused lightness into her tone, but her reluctance to incite another row didn't mean she was damping down what was important to her.

'No doubt you found your usual diplomatic way to deny my existence despite it being an open secret,' he returned with a distinct edge to his tone.

Sienna's breath snagged in her lungs. Yes, the subject was definitely still a sore one. But one she intended to tackle soon. Maybe tonight...

'I've never denied your existence. Merely not fuelled workplace gossip. There's a difference.'

His upper lip curled slightly, his jaw flexing a touch. 'If you say so.'

She floundered for a moment, the ground beneath her feet shaking a little. Was her continued denial of their relationship outside the privacy of their penthouse causing more damage than she realised?

Inhaling deeply, she widened her smile.

'I do say so. And it would've been perfect if you'd been

here, regardless of who knows about us.' Sienna knew she was offering a tentative olive branch, while subtly digging for answers to questions she wasn't completely certain were wise to pursue, but the worry that had taken root between her ribs was growing by the second.

'I'm sorry. The situation couldn't be helped.'

She wasn't surprised at the slightly cryptic answer. The enigma that was Emiliano Castillo operated at optimum capacity, always. She'd learned the hard way that to gain his attention she had to meet her lover and boss toe to toe. It was what had brought her to his attention in the boardroom. It was why their chemistry remained sizzling hot in the bedroom. A chemistry that had stunned and bewildered her in the beginning and continued to overawe her even now. It was the reason she checked herself now from leaving the safety of the mantel to close the seemingly yawning distance between them, even though every muscle strained to be in his arms.

Denying herself the pleasure, she remained where she was, sensing the deep, puzzling tension within him as a muscle jumped in his shadowed cheek. But even from a distance she experienced the jolt of electricity that lanced through her when his eyes remained fixed on hers. 'You didn't elaborate on what was going on. Is it Matias?' she asked.

A shadow drifted over his face. 'In a way, yes.'

'Is he okay? Has there been any improve—'

'His condition remains unchanged,' he interrupted.

Her gaze dropped, drifting over his lower lip. He inhaled sharply, gratifying her with his reaction. But his hands remained in his pockets.

'So you spent all six days with your parents?'

Another clench of his jaw. '*Sí.*' The word was chillingly grave.

Her heart dropped. 'Emiliano...I... Is everything okay?'

He finally breached the gap between them and grasped her hand in his. Lowering their linked hands, he stared at her upturned palm for several seconds before he released her. 'No, everything is not okay, but it's nothing that won't resolve itself eventually.'

She opened her mouth and started to demand more information. But he'd turned away.

'Come, the food will be getting cold.'

She followed him into the dining room and pinned the smile on her face as he held her chair and saw her seated. Again she anticipated his touch on her bare shoulders, a drift of his sensual mouth across her temple. She received neither.

She watched him take his own seat, the neutrality of his expression underlined with a grimness that lodged a cold stone in her stomach.

'Emiliano…'

'I belayed ordering oysters. I didn't want them to be ruined in transit. We'll have your second favourite.'

She waved him away as he opened the first of the specially packed gourmet dishes. 'It's fine. I don't care about the food. We can have oysters some other time.' Her blush at the mention of oysters and the special significance they held for them was suppressed beneath the blooming disquiet. Even then she couldn't help but be disturbed that he'd made the order without speaking to her first. 'Tell me what's going on.'

His firm mouth thinned for a split second and the eyes that met hers were closed off, bordering on cold. '*Querida*, I don't wish to upset your birthday celebration.'

She frowned. 'Why would telling me how your trip went ruin my birthday? What happened?' she pressed.

His gaze swept away from hers, back to the dish in his hand. Shutting her out. 'My parents happened.' He looked up, tawny-gold eyes piercing her. 'And since they come under the numerous subjects we don't discuss, perhaps we can drop it?' he drawled.

The statement hurt a little, but Sienna couldn't deny that it was accurate. There were swathes of their private lives they avoided, their common threads of familiarity were business and the bedroom. Again she experienced the ominous sense of shifting sands, prompting her to go against her better judgment.

'Maybe…this one time we can make an exception? And, before you bite my head off, I only request it because I can see that whatever happened is affecting you, Emiliano.'

'You are kind, *querida*, but I would also caution you against making those sorts of statements. There are some things you can't take back. Besides, I believe you're exaggerating things a little.' He dished the seafood salad starter onto her plate, served himself and poured them both glasses of chilled white wine.

'You think I'm exaggerating things?' She hated herself for the tiny catch in her voice and the needy words that spilled in the bid to make her point. 'Then why haven't you kissed me since you walked in the door? Usually, you can't keep your hands off me, yet you haven't so much as touched me. And, if you clench your jaw any tighter, it'll snap.'

'I've told you, you look breathtaking. I've wished you happy birthday. I showered you with presents all day, even in my absence. Perhaps I'm saving the rest for later. I know how much you love the anticipation,' he drawled before he raised his glass to her and took a large gulp.

Sienna caught a glimpse of the banked desire in his eyes. Her heart resumed its erratic thumping, but she couldn't dismiss the other, more terrifying feeling residing beneath her breast. Because there was something else lurking in his eyes. Something cold, bracing and soul threatening.

'Six days of anticipation is more than enough. "One day

is too long." Isn't that what you said last month when you returned from that two-day business summit in Athens?'

That she had to remind him of that was even more shocking, the unusual recounting of gestures received but never spoken about making her reel.

'Careful, Sienna, or you'll have me thinking these declarations you've previously led me to believe are over the top are in fact secretly yearned for.'

A flush crept up her neck to stain her cheeks but she didn't drop her gaze. 'As I said, perhaps I wish to make an exception.'

His shrug was almost...bored. 'There is no need. I've had a long and turbulent flight, *amante*. Right now, I want to relax and see you sated with food. Is that too much to ask?' His voice held a definite bite. A warning to leave well enough alone.

She shook her head, convinced more than ever that something was seriously wrong. 'Whatever it is that's bothering you, I...I want to help.' Throwing caution to the wind, she abandoned her glass and, in a first move that made her insides quake, she initiated touch by placing her hand over his.

He tensed, his nostrils flaring as he gazed down at her hand.

Then he removed his hand from under hers.

Her heart stopped as another thought sliced through her mind.

'Emiliano? Is it me?'

The eyes that held hers were completely devoid of emotion. 'Sienna, leave this alone...'

'Oh, God, are you annoyed with me for finalising the Younger deal without you?'

'What?'

'You gave me carte blanche, remember? You said I should go ahead and offer whatever we needed to land the deal. And that's what I did. I know it was another five million more than we initially agreed, but I did the figures and judged that it was worth it.'

His brow clamped in a frown as he yanked his tie loose with his free hand. '*Santo cielo*, not everything is about business—' He ruthlessly checked himself and drew in a breath. 'Rest assured, I'm not annoyed with you about the deal. Without your quick thinking and acting, we'd have lost it. I believe I had Denise send you an email commending you for it today.'

She'd seen the email from his executive assistant, and again wondered why Emiliano hadn't contacted her himself. 'Okay, but—'

'You want further commendations from me? More flowers? More accolades on top of the presents you've already received? Is that what this show of neediness is about?'

Shock and anger scythed equal swathes of pain through her. 'Excuse me?' Despite having called herself the same only minutes ago, the label stung badly.

He drained his glass and set it down with more force than necessary. Charging to his feet, he rounded the table. His impressive height and bristling demeanour would've made a lesser woman cower. Hell, she'd seen grown men wither beneath the look displayed on his face now.

But she'd never been one of them.

Surging to her feet, she faced him, their untouched food abandoned. 'Did you just call me *needy*?'

'Am I wrong? Now that we're behind closed doors, where your precious reputation isn't at risk, do you not *need* something from me? Have you not been full of *needful* words since I walked in the door?' he accused.

'Don't twist my words. I just want to talk to you, find out what's—'

'I don't want to *talk*, *querida*. You're usually adept at

picking up simple cues like that. Has my absence affected you that much, or is there another agenda going on here?' he taunted.

The tightly furled subject she'd tentatively intended to broach with him tonight knotted harder, congealing into stone that chafed against her heart. Incisive eyes dragged over her face, probing her expression and then widening upon witnessing the evidence she couldn't quite disguise.

'*Si*, another agenda,' he bit out. 'Do I get three guesses or shall I strike for gold and deduce that you're breaking your *unique* mould to broach the predictable "where do we go from here?" conversation women feel the *need* to have at the most inappropriate times?'

Sienna wasn't sure whether it was his uncanny acuity or the abrasive tone that alarmed her more. 'You're turning this around on me, Emiliano. We were talking about you.'

'A subject I've clearly expressed my abhorrence for. Now, are we to go around in circles, or are we going to eat?'

She lifted her chin, the distress and foreboding she'd staunched so fiercely blooming into life within her chest. 'I've lost my appetite.'

He took another dangerous step closer, swallowing the gap between them, extinguishing the very air that sustained them until only pure, sizzling electricity remained. Soot-coloured lashes swept down and paused, the heat in his eyes branding her mouth for endless seconds before his gaze rose again.

'For food? Or for everything else?' His voice was thicker. Deeper. His nostrils flared in blatant, carnal hunger.

'Why are you so angry with me?' she whispered, unable to stem the dread crawling over her skin.

An enigmatic expression blanketed his face for a blind second, his eyes blazing with a light she couldn't fathom. 'Perhaps I'm tired of being compartmentalised in your life, of being put on a shelf and taken down and dusted off only when your needs get the better of you.'

She gasped. 'What? I've never—'

The firm finger that drifted over her lower lip stemmed her answer. 'I wish to get off this merry-go-round. So I ask you again, what have you lost your appetite for?'

Lust, need, anger and hurt strangled her in equal measures. With a few pithy words, he'd reduced her to a needy female eager to sink her talons into a man she wanted to possess. With one label, he'd reminded her of the one thing she'd vowed never to be again.

Dependent.

They'd had disagreements before, but nothing like this. Sienna couldn't catch her breath, couldn't stem the hurt that flowed like a bloodied wound. But with each second that passed, with each intake of his breath and exhalation of hers, a different emotion surged forth. Familiar. Overwhelming. Devastating.

A deep tremble seized her, shaking her from head to toe. He saw her reaction and triumph coated his features, his eyes darkening as he watched. Waited.

'Emiliano…'

'*Sí*, Sienna?' he whispered against her mouth, but holding himself a breath away, taunting her with his proximity.

Her breath shook out. 'Something's going on. Don't make me think I'm crazy or that I'm overreacting. Please, just tell me—'

'Stop. You know better than to push a closed subject. You're an expert on closed subjects, after all. So do not let tonight be the moment you change your tune, *querida*, hmm?'

Another bolt of shock went through her. Her gaze collided with his. The hunger was still there, but everything else was just…wrong. 'Who *are* you? Why are you speaking to me this way?'

'You're the one who insists on incessant discourse,' he bit out at her.

'You don't want me to talk? Fine!' She grabbed his tie and pulled it free. One vicious twist of her wrist sent it flying across the polished table. Then she attacked his shirt. Buttons turned into tiny missiles launched across the room, the depth of unbelievable hurt and lust tearing through her and making her irrational.

Her actions felt surreal, an out-of-body experience that sent shockwaves through her other self, the one observing what she was doing from a safe distance.

The live, breathing one initiating hot-headed moves swallowed hard at the first sight of Emiliano's tanned, chiselled chest and gave a helpless groan, her body weakening and surging with desire at the same time.

Emiliano's breath hissed out when she reached for his belt buckle. *'Querida—'*

'No! If I don't get to talk, neither do you,' she insisted, probably because she was terrified that talking now would force her to think about what she was doing, and the possible reason behind Emiliano's behaviour. Which was wrong, but she couldn't help it. Not in this instance. Not when a mere hour ago she'd felt on top of the world.

Her fingers gained renewed power. Tugging the belt free, she jerked it away and heard it whistle through the loops on its way across the floor. Her fingers brushed the powerful erection behind his fly and a powerful shudder rocked him.

'Dios mio, Sienna…' His voice was thick, his arousal present and potent.

'Unless, of course, you're going to tell me I'm crazy to think you want me?' She kicked away her shoes and reached for the zipper of her dress. Lowered it. Watched the tops of his sculptured cheekbones flush with raw need.

His lips parted, his breath emerging in shallow pants

as he watched her dress loosen and drape, secured only by her heaving breasts.

But, as quickly as the alien bravado had risen, it died, leaving her once again flailing, distraught.

What on earth was she doing?

Dropping her hands, she hiked up the skirt of the gown and took one step back, then another. He followed, tracking her with the calculated steps of a ravenous predator.

They moved like that, locked in their erotic dance, out of the dining room. Somewhere along the way, the top part of her dress dropped, exposing her.

Emiliano stumbled. Then cursed under his breath. At any other time, Sienna would've smiled a wicked, teasing smile. Not now. Now each breath was weighted with desire, yes, but also with a fearful heaviness that left little room for hilarity.

'Am I crazy, Emiliano?' she pressed, even though part of her desperately urged herself to remain silent.

Long seconds ticked by as he prowled after her. Her back touched the bedroom door, swinging it open. Momentarily, his gaze flicked past her to the king-sized bed they'd shared insanely passionate moments in for six months. The eyes that returned to meet hers were heavy with need and regret. Whether it was for their argument or for something else, she didn't know. Although, with the ache in her chest she couldn't quite shift, she suspected the latter.

CHAPTER TWO

'No, you're not crazy.'

The strained admission restored a little of her hurt. As did the slightly desperate aura about him as he nudged her backwards into the bedroom. Whatever else was going on, Emiliano still wanted her. It was by no means anywhere near what she ultimately wanted from him, but the knowledge soothed and settled the wild alarm racing through her veins. A little restored feminine power would sustain her. For now.

Tomorrow. She'd revisit the subject again tomorrow. Once they'd slaked far more immediate and urgent needs. Even though it went against her nature to leave a problem untackled, she would refrain from pushing for answers tonight.

With that thought, she let go of her dress. It pooled to the floor a mere second before Emiliano pounced, lifting her out of it to stand her naked except for her thong and his jewels. His arms dropped back to his sides, and she watched his hands clench with electric tension for a ragged second, then jerk towards her, beckoning her forward, his eyes burning gold. 'Come here, Sienna.'

Invitation of the most sinful nature. Invitation she grasped with both hands, stumbling forward into his arms.

Hard hands plastered her against his body and tangled in her hair, holding her still before she could satisfy the urgent need to kiss him.

He stared down at her, eyes endless pools of shadows, secrets and passion. But between one second and the next, she once again caught a glimpse of something that made her heart clench.

'Emiliano…'

He nudged her even closer, heat from his body chopping off her words, the disturbing look in his eyes resolutely erased. 'Take what you need, my little wildcat,' he breathed against her mouth.

With a moan, she rose on tiptoe, her hands sliding around his neck as her mouth pressed gloriously, ravenously, against his. Her eyes slid shut, the better to savour what she'd missed, what she'd craved so desperately, these past six days. Her senses sang when his hands wrapped tighter, mercilessly, around her, his deep groan relaying his mutual feelings.

Tongues meshing, relishing, devouring, the kiss deepened, their ragged breathing the only sound in the room as he walked her backwards on plush carpet, his aim the wide bed which was their personal haven.

Sienna gripped him tighter as he swept her off her feet and placed her on the bed. When he attempted to move, to shed the rest of his clothes, she stopped him, the idea of letting him go bringing a fresh wave of alarm.

If her unusually possessive hold on him registered, he didn't give an indication. Instead, he rolled them sideways, still delivering hot, pleasurable kisses as he impatiently shucked off shoes and trousers. His briefs followed and her breath caught all over again at the heat of his girth against her thigh.

Greedy hands closed over his steely hardness. They both groaned. Oh, how she'd longed for this.

'I missed you. So much!' she gasped between kisses, once again letting go of the tight hold she usually held on her emotions.

His body grew tauter, the carnal tension whipped through him, making muscles and sinew rock-hard beneath her touch. She expected him to reply with something wickedly decadent. His clever tongue would usually by now be whispering erotically charged words in her ear.

He remained silent even as his hands moved feverishly over her body.

Her often vocal, always possessive lover was choosing mute seduction, delivering his pleasure through his hands and mouth, ruthlessly dragging double bliss with harder kisses and rougher caresses. Sienna thrilled to the exchange even as she pushed back the million *whys* that demanded answering.

His tongue slid over her skin, tasting her nipples, sucking, teasing, melting her thoughts, to leave only pure sensation. A firm tug at her hips ripped free her panties, then he was there, at the centre of her need, delivering even more potent bliss. She sank her fingers into his hair, her cries growing louder as pleasure piled upon pleasure. Until it culminated in endless waves of ecstasy.

Sienna was still floating when he parted her thighs wider, filling her senses with his presence. Prying her eyes open, she stared at the god whose intellect and charisma left her in awe, whose touch lifted her from ordinary to extraordinary.

Who was staring at her with narrowed eyes even more shadowed than they had been minutes ago. Before she could attempt to voice her quaking thoughts, he slanted his mouth over hers and penetrated her in one smooth, urgent thrust.

Flung straight back to nirvana, Sienna could only hold on as she was completely, utterly possessed. Nails bit into flesh, cries turned into screams. Emiliano pushed her to the brink over and over, slowing down just before she reached her peak. As if he wanted their lovemaking to go on for ever. As if he wanted to be imprinted on her very soul.

As if he wanted the experience to be unforgettable.

Why?

The word blazed across her mind again, larger, louder. Her hands shook as she framed his face, searching his eyes.

'Emiliano…please…' she whispered.

His jaw turned to stone beneath her fingers. With a thick grunt, he pulled out of her body, flipped her onto her stomach and surged back into her. Brushing her hair out of the way, he sank his teeth into her nape, roughly tasting her, branding her. Raw pleasure ploughed through her, leaving her clawing at the sheets as another orgasm surged high.

Behind her, she heard his rough breathing, his own impending climax bearing down on him. She wanted to hold him in her arms, look into his eyes and be reassured that everything was all right between them. Or as near enough as possible.

Because, although it had hurt to have him point it out, she knew their relationship had a few inescapable flaws. Flaws that seemed to gape wider with each passing second. Flaws she needed to address.

But he had her pinned, six feet three inches of superior masculinity spread all over her delivering sensation she never wanted to end. So, closing her eyes, Sienna gave in, diving headlong into pure heaven as stars exploded across her vision.

Endless minutes later, when their bodies had cooled and their breathing calmed, he slid off her and gathered her in his arms.

Strong fingers slid into her hair, the movement unusually jerky. His gaze was hooded when it met hers, hiding his expression.

'Happy birthday,' he rasped.

'I…' She floundered for a second, wondering whether to go back on her resolution and tread the dangerous waters swirling beneath her feet.

'Emiliano…'

'These look exquisite on you.' He pulled her closer, his fingers slipping down to trace the skin beneath the diamond necklace even as the forbidding force of his stare punched holes in her resolve.

Tomorrow, she decided once again. 'Thank you,' she murmured.

Tilting her head up, he placed a hard, short kiss on her swollen lips. 'Sleep now,' he ordered.

In the aftermath of bliss and even with her mind churning, Sienna couldn't hold back the drugging effect of that command. So she gave in.

What felt like only minutes later, she jerked upright, her heart hammering. Beside her, Emiliano was lost in slumber, one muscled arm curved over his head. Heart twisting, she studied him, vainly trying to decipher what was wrong. In sleep, his breathtakingly handsome face was less forbidding, his jaw slightly slack and his forehead smooth. She didn't deem him any less intimidating but at least she could stare at him now without the bracing force field that usually surrounded him. She even dared to lift a hand to his full lower lip, tracing the velvet-smooth skin. He exhaled harshly in his sleep and she froze. Withdrawing her fingers, she lay back, knowing sleep was out of the question with her mind once again in churn mode.

Half an hour later, she gave up and rose from the bed. At 5:30 a.m. in early November, it was still dark outside. Going for a run outside in the dark without Emiliano would incur his displeasure, as she'd found out on the one occasion she'd attempted to do so. In fact, he'd completely banned her from running outside without him. But she needed physical exertion to prevent her from waking him up and demanding to know what was going on.

Quietly tugging on her running gear in the large dressing room adjoining the master suite, she silently let herself out and took the lift down to the basement, where the top-line gym reserved for the exclusive use of the penthouse owners was located. Plugging in her earbuds, she hit the treadmill, running at her top speed for a solid hour before her leaden legs forced her to slow down.

When she stepped off the machine, her resolution was firmly back in place, her mind no longer racing. Emiliano valued her professionally because she wasn't afraid to go after tough, seemingly unattainable deals. It was what had seen her rise from junior fund manager to junior vice-president in the three years she'd been with his venture capitalist firm.

While privately her lack of sexual experience placed her somewhat on a back foot, she'd never let Emiliano cow her. She was also brave enough to admit her new but secret emotions also factored in whatever situation was brewing between them. Which was why she would tackle it now.

Setting down the bottle of mineral water she'd rehydrated from, she left the basement via the stairs. She would pick up the newspapers and magazines they had delivered to the penthouse to prevent their talk from being interrupted by the concierge.

She reached the ground floor and crossed the polished marble foyer to the concierge desk. Exchanging a greeting with the manager, she accepted the stack and crossed to the lift. The other tiny secret she'd been harbouring for several weeks lightened her heart a little as she entered the carriage and pressed the button.

Having witnessed the pleased light in Emiliano's eyes whenever she'd responded in Spanish to a simple question, she'd embraced the idea to take it further.

She hadn't divulged her attempt to learn Spanish to Emiliano because she'd wanted to approach the outskirts of proficiency before she told him. Privately, she'd devoured Spanish newspapers and magazines in her spare time in the hope of quickly learning her lover's mother tongue, and even admitted that it had become a guilty pleasure to gorge on all things Argentinian.

Unfortunately, it was the reason the headline screaming from the front page of the glossy celebrity magazine made perfect sense to her once she fished it out of the pile.

Stumbling out of her lift, she froze to a halt, her heart dropping to her toes. Unable to catch her breath, she stared, first at the photo, then back at the headline.

A Castillo-Cabrera Union!

The rest of the papers fell out of her hand, her useless limbs unable to hang on to anything but the evidence of all her *whys* spelled out in bold white letters. Her shocked eyes dropped to the smaller print.

The Polo Match Made in Heaven!

Emiliano Castillo to Wed Graciela Cabrera.

There were other words, such as *wedding of the year... Dynastic union... Valentine's Day wedding...*

But her vision was blurring, her heart refusing to pump properly. She was going to pass out. She was sure of it. She wasn't sure whether to view her present state as a blessing. What she did know was that she wanted to block out the sight of Emiliano and the drop-dead gorgeous caramel blonde sitting at the intimate candlelit table, her hand on top of his, her smile holding a thousand delicious secrets as she stared at him.

And he stared back at her.

He wasn't smiling—Emiliano *never* smiled in the presence of a camera, especially one wielded by a paparazzo. Most of the time he glared at the intrusion. He wasn't glaring this time. The expression on his face was even...accommodating. Fond.

Lungs burning, Sienna forced herself to take a breath. Turn the pages. Her world turning to ash, she stared at glossy page after glossy page of Emiliano and his new *amor*. On the fifth page, she stared, tears surging into her eyes, at the ring on the finger which announced Graciela Cabrera as the brand new fiancée of Emiliano Castillo.

To add insult to injury, her heart tripped to a stop when she saw what Emiliano was wearing. If there was even a shadow of a doubt that this picture was a terrible, cruel hoax, it was wiped clean when she saw the tie. She'd gifted that tie to him on his birthday two months ago— had packed it in his suitcase herself exactly one week ago, when she'd sent him off with a kiss on his lips and hope in her heart. She was world-wise enough to know sometimes the tabloid media regurgitated old photos and manipulated images to suit their headline. The evidence of the tie confirmed these pictures weren't fakes.

Finally, *everything* about last night...about the past few days' silence...made sense.

She stumbled forward, the scattered papers forgotten as she made her way back inside, absently wondering how she was able to put one foot in front of the other when she felt so numb.

Time and space ceased to make sense until she was standing before the bedroom doors. Her hand shook as she raised it to the handle. She clenched her fist tight in a desperate bid to retain some control. She had to confront this, in spite of what the outcome would be.

Had to.

She jerked at the forceful wrench of the door from the inside, stealing away the control she'd barely summoned. Emiliano stopped short before her, his face in a deep frown.

'Sienna, what are you doing standing...?'

She stared at him. He was right there in front of her. Powerful. Magnetically charismatic. Drop-dead gorgeous.

Bastard.

She didn't want to look at him. Dear God, it hurt just

to lift her gaze to meet his. Because even now she wanted desperately to cling to the hope that she'd got it wrong. That the pictures in the magazine clutched in her fist, his lack of emails, his coldly forbidding expression upon his return, even his silent lovemaking, had all been in her imagination.

But she met his gaze. And knew she was clinging to false hope.

'Is it true?' she tried asking anyway. One last time.

Tawny gold eyes hardened a touch, the coldness returning. 'Is what true?'

A bolt of anger freed her frozen limbs. 'Don't play games with me, Emiliano. It's beneath—'

She'd been about to say *us*. Except there was no *us* any more. Had there ever been? Her frantic brain raced, desperately sifting, analysing every gesture, every word, wondering if everything she'd lived, revelled in and hoped for during their relationship had been based on a colossal lie.

'This!' She shoved the magazine into the bare steel torso draped with the navy blue shirt he'd been about to button. *'Is it true you're engaged?'*

Ripping off her MP4 player and earphones, she dropped them onto a nearby dresser and turned, watching him flip through the pages before tossing the magazine aside.

The eyes that met hers were arrogantly unapologetic. 'Yes.'

The last minute's anger had fooled her into thinking she was strong, that she could withstand whatever was coming her way.

She was wrong.

The punch to her solar plexus from his words robbed her of breath and weakened her knees. Shaking her head, she stared at him. Waited for him to continue. He didn't. He just stared back at her, his expression icily neutral.

'"Yes"? That's all you're going to say?'

He braced strong hands on lean hips, his stance cold and withdrawn. 'You're in no condition to hear any more right now—'

'Are you serious? So what, you expect me to just…go through my day until you *deem* me ready?' Incredulity rendered her voice hoarse and shaky.

'I would prefer to have this conversation with you when you're not emotionally high-strung, *sí*,' he rasped before raising his hands to begin buttoning his shirt.

Inhaling long and slow, Sienna fought for the control she was so good at attaining in the workplace. Except this wasn't work. This was so much more. 'You owe me an explanation. Right now. Or are you too much of a coward to grant me one?'

He froze, hard eyes lancing into her with the brutal force of a scalpel. 'Watch your tone with me, *querida*,' he warned.

'Do not call me that! You just told me you're engaged to another woman. Engaged! And you dare to call me your *darling*?'

A puzzled expression flicked like lightning over his face, as if he didn't understand her objection. Then it was gone and he was back to the stranger who'd walked into their penthouse twelve hours ago.

Her green eyes flashed. 'Were you seeing her behind my back?'

A black frown clamped his forehead as he secured the last button. 'I do not cheat.'

'No? You've never cheated? What was last night, then? Weren't you cheating on *her* with *me*?'

'You're my lover. She knows of our association. She understands that it needs to be taken care of.'

'Oh, how very accommodating of her. And is that what you were doing last night? *Taking care of me* before you dumped me?'

He jerked back, as if she'd struck him. 'Sienna, you need to calm—'

'You couldn't resist one last tumble between the sheets before you handed me my marching orders?'

He had the grace to look uncomfortable. 'It was your birthday…'

Hot pins stabbed her until she was a whisper away from howling. It was too much to take standing still. So she paced. 'How decent of you. I was the poor, pathetic soon-to-be ex-lover you couldn't stand to disappoint on her birthday, so you waited for me to find out what you'd been up to from the press?'

He slammed the cufflinks he'd picked up back onto the dresser. '*Basta!* This wasn't how I intended to break the news.'

'How very inconvenient for you!'

He pinched the bridge of his nose and inhaled deeply. 'I'm heading to the office now—I have a conference call scheduled with Norway which has been postponed twice. But let's catch up later. Maybe this evening? I don't mind if you take the day off to absorb the news. Then, tonight, we can talk about this rationally.'

'About the fact that you were going on a trip to see your parents but went and got engaged instead?'

His jaws gritted together for a second. 'Amongst other things, yes.'

She forced herself to stop. To face him. 'Fine, let's have it. Surely I'm worth five minutes of your time right now?'

'I don't think—'

'I do!'

Taking a deep breath, he stared at her. 'Sienna, it wasn't supposed to happen this way.'

'What wasn't? Please spell it out fully so I understand.'

One sleek eyebrow rose as if he was seeing her in a new

light. In that moment, Sienna wasn't sure she wanted to find out what he saw as he stared at her.

'The way you're reacting right now, I'm almost tempted to believe your career *isn't* more important to you than this thing between us, whereas I know for a fact that, if I asked you to choose, you wouldn't even blink before choosing the former.'

She inhaled sharply. 'First of all, if we ever found ourselves in the position of you asking me to choose, then we'd be in serious trouble, especially when I know how many female, family-orientated executives you employ. Which makes me think this would most probably be some sort of test. Why would you need to do that, Emiliano?'

He shrugged, but the gleam she'd witnessed in his eyes last night burned even brighter this morning. 'Perhaps the idea of coming second best doesn't sit well with me. Perhaps I'm thoroughly bored of it.'

Shocked laughter spilled from her lips. '*Second best? How… When…*have you ever allowed yourself to come second best? You win at absolutely everything!'

His lids swept down, his mouth twisting. 'That is where you're wrong.'

'Fine. Maybe we don't know each other as well as we should, but I guess you not even bothering to give me any option speaks volumes!'

He slashed a hand through his hair. 'I was going to give you… *Dios*, this wasn't how…I have to do this.'

She stilled, the combination of Emiliano struggling for words and the choice of those words unsettling her. 'You *have* to?'

'*Si*, I gave my word.'

'Your word? To *who*?'

He huffed, a breath filled with icy frustration. 'It's a family thing. I don't know enough about your own family circumstances, since you've never felt quite like sharing, so I will forgive you if you don't understand.'

That cut her off at the knees. 'How dare you?' She gasped, raw pain hammering her from heart to soul. 'You've equally withheld your own background from me. Don't punish me for thinking I was respecting your wishes. And, whatever my circumstances, you can't assume that I don't understand the concept of family.' Being an orphan had triggered a yearning for a family of her own, a wish she held dear in her heart, the fulfilment of that dream a hope she refused to give up.

Emiliano's mouth thinned. 'You mistook my meaning.'

'Looks like I've mistaken a lot of things. Things like you neglecting to tell me you've been *promised* to some-body else all along.'

'I'm not. I wasn't.'

'Then what is this?' She indicated the paper. 'Don't in-sult my intelligence. You know her. There's a familiarity there, so something must have been going on.'

'Our families are…connected. I've known her since she was a child.'

'And they needed a marriage, so you agreed to step in?' she mocked with a pained laugh.

Laughter that dried up when he nodded.

'Yes, something like that.'

She gasped. 'You're serious.'

He didn't blink. 'I'm serious.'

Her mouth dropped open, but no words emerged. Shak-ing her head, she tried to clear the buzzing growing louder.

'I'm going to go out on a limb and mention that there is another scenario I was thinking about for us in light of this news.'

He stared at her, a touch of something she absurdly wanted to label uncertainty flashing across his face before it disappeared. When her vocal cords refused to work, he continued, 'If you want our…liaison to continue, I'm willing to discuss how we—'

A punch of rage freed up her vocal cords. 'I sincerely hope you're not about to suggest I be your bit on the side while you're married to someone else!'

His face hardened into a rigid mask of fury. 'Please refrain from putting words in my mouth.'

She folded her arms. 'Okay, I'm listening.'

He started to speak, then clenched his jaw again and shook his head. 'Perhaps discretion is the better part of valour here. I'll be speaking to my lawyers this morning. You can keep the penthouse and everything in it. I'll have the requisite deeds drawn up. Also one of the cars. Pick whichever one you please. If you want anything else, let me know. I'll try and accommodate—'

'Are you discussing *possessions* with me, Emiliano? I want to know why you're engaged to another woman when you're supposed to be mine!' She was shouting, her pain raw and unfettered, her dignity in shreds. But she couldn't help it.

And with each word she flung at him he grew colder, withdrawing into a block of marble. Retrieving his cufflinks, he slotted them into place with calm, precise movements. 'I thought there could be a…negotiation…but it's clear I was wrong.'

Her hands splayed out in a bracing gesture, appealing for understanding in a world gone crazy. 'A *negotiation*? What on earth are you talking about?'

'It doesn't matter now. I didn't take this decision lightly, but it's done, Sienna. For the immediate future there'll be no changing it. It's clear that dissecting it wouldn't be productive to you. Not in this moment, anyway. Perhaps not ever,' he stated with a finality that chilled her to the bone.

'So that's it? I'm dumped with no proper explanation?'

He stared at her for endless seconds. 'Whether we want

to admit it or not, we were both aware this thing between us was bound to run its course sooner or later. Maybe it's better that it's sooner.'

Then he picked up his jacket and walked out the door.

CHAPTER THREE

THE NEXT FEW hours were spent in a semifugue state. Sadly, Sienna wasn't numb enough to remain painfully unaware of what was happening.

Her voice was hoarse as she called out to Emiliano. His stone-cold silence as he left the penthouse. Her cracking voice as she instructed her secretary to push her appointments to later in the day.

The deep concern on Alfie's face when she refused breakfast and asked him to procure packing boxes, and the endless waves of bewildered agony as she stuffed her belongings into boxes and suitcases, organised storage facilities and booked herself into a hotel.

Tears. So many heart-shredding, despised tears as she stood in the shower in a soulless hotel room, hating herself for not being stronger, excruciatingly aware she'd let herself slide into the danger zone of false hope based on useless foundations. But, as she dried off and dressed, she also recognised the slow build of anger. Of determination.

She'd put every safeguard in place to protect herself, yet she'd let herself hope, just as she had as a child staring yearningly out of the orphanage window for something *better*, when she'd known better should first and foremost come from herself. From *within*. She'd allowed herself to forget her history, to be lulled into disabling the locked-in belief that abandonment by those she let close was a thing of the past. She'd let herself indulge in fantasies built around a man who'd made it clear from his previous relationships that he would never settle down.

But he had settled.

What was an engagement, if not a precursor to the ultimate commitment?

But he didn't choose you, remember? Like your own mother chose a different life without you.

She tried to fortify herself against the savage pain the reminder brought. But she felt it like a raw wound exposed to salt, and couldn't stem the harrowing memories of growing up in an orphanage, the heartbreak each time a hoped-for foster family rejected her or, even worse, gave her the initial promise of a family only to yank it away weeks or months later.

She should have been used to rejection by now. Should've kept her steel-plated armour securely fastened in place. Instead, she'd let Emiliano in.

The ramifications of her stupidity held her hostage as she left the hotel and hailed a cab to what had once been a place of pride for her achievements and was now the secondary scene of her downfall.

As she walked through the grand, breathtaking marble-and-glass lobby of the Castillo Tower in the city, Sienna couldn't help but feel that, despite her staunchest effort to keep her private life under wraps, every gaze directed her way held a degree of mocking judgement of the poor choices she'd made.

Her secretary's furtive gaze and normally exuberant but now-hushed tone told Sienna her disguise had failed.

Or was it because news of Emiliano's engagement had already filtered through? Of course. Castillo Ventures, no matter how progressive a work place, was still a hotbed of interoffice gossip. She didn't doubt that every single member of the five-hundred-strong workforce would know the truth by now, although her stellar but straitlaced reputation would mean no one would say anything to her face.

Fresh pain battered her as she walked into her office and shut the door. On shaky legs, she approached her desk and sank behind it. Fingers trembling, she pulled up the requisite programme, typed a brief, succinct letter and sent it.

Ignoring the loud pings of emails that dropped into her inbox, she calmly set a notepad and pen on the desk before her and got on with planning for her future. For as long as she could remember, having a plan in place had helped keep her focus true. She'd only abandoned that plan when a dynamic, drop-dead gorgeous Argentinian had set her in his sights and piled on relentless pressure, leading her to imagine mistakenly that he was her future.

It was time to relocate her compass.

Ignoring the phone when it began to ring, she meticulously set out her to-do list, starting with finding a place to live.

Ten minutes later, she heard the soft rap on her door, followed by her secretary's entrance. When she didn't immediately speak, Sienna forced her heavy head up, frowning when she saw Laura's visible distress.

'Yes, what is it?'

'Um… Mr Castillo wants to see you.'

Her heart stuttered, then dropped to her stomach. Somehow, she managed a tight smile. 'Please let him know I'm busy. I have work to do.'

'I… He said you're to drop whatever you're doing and report to his office right away.'

'Tell him—'

'I'm sorry, Sienna,' her secretary interrupted, naked apprehension on her usually cheery face. 'I know you said you don't want to be disturbed, but he's been calling you for the last five minutes. He made it clear he wants you in his office. He said to let him know when you're on your way. And that he will hold me responsible if you don't come right away.'

Rage boiling in her gut, she surged to her feet just as her phone rang again. She didn't need to look down to confirm the caller's identity. 'It's okay, Laura. I'll deal with it.'

Her secretary was barely out of the door when she snatched up the phone. 'I'd thank you not to threaten my secretary.'

'She's my employee. If you didn't want her put in this position then you should have picked up your phone when I called.'

'What do you want, Mr Castillo?' She strove for a calm, poised tone and shut her eyes briefly in relief when she achieved it.

At the end of the line, Emiliano didn't respond for a few terse seconds. 'What I wanted when I called ten minutes ago. You, in my office. Now.'

'I'm—'

'Not as busy as you say. You forget I have access to your diary. Come now, Sienna. Or I'll come down there. My office affords us more privacy than yours, but either way you and I will be doing this face-to-face. The location is your choice. You have three minutes.' The line went dead.

Her hands shook as she hung up. Anger still rumbled in her belly, but the thought of seeing him again so soon meant a different kind of emotion—pain and loss for what she'd never really had superseded that anger, holding her immobile in her chair for a long moment before she forced herself to move.

Hushed whispers and quickly muted conversations trailed her as she made her way to the lift. For a wild, absurd second she wished she'd relocated her office from the twentieth to the thirtieth floor at Emiliano's bidding two months ago. But she swiftly conceded it would've been ten times worse to be in her situation now.

Either way was no consolation. So she put one foot in front of the other until she stood before a set of misted glass double doors. Emiliano's trusted PA was nowhere in sight. Whether by coincidence or by design, she didn't give herself time to dwell on it as she turned the handle and pushed the door open.

He sat at his smoked-glass desk, the iconic vista of the financial heart of London sprawled out behind him. He'd shed the jacket to his bespoke suit. Or perhaps he'd never worn it. His pinstriped tie was loosened, the top button of his shirt undone and his hair sexily dishevelled, as if he'd run his hand through it several times.

Not quite his usual impeccable, well put-together self. But the package was no less impactful. A direct hit to her severely flailing senses, especially when he raised his arrogant head, locked those gold eyes on her and tracked her approach.

She stopped a good distance from his desk, stepping deeper into his orbit, breathing him in… No. Better she stay where she was for her self-preservation, which was way past overdue for reinforcement.

'You wanted to see me. Here I am.'

Narrowed eyes tracked her from head to toe. 'Why are you wearing black? You know how much I hate it when you do.'

She refused to allow memories surrounding discussions of her clothes to intrude. Most of them had taken place in their once-shared dressing room when they'd been naked. 'You didn't summon me to discuss my work gear. That would be a colossal waste of both our time.'

'I asked you here to discuss this.' He waved a large, expressive hand at his computer screen, his jaw as tight as the pellet-hard words falling from his lips. 'What is the meaning of it?'

'If you're referring to my resignation letter, I would've thought it was self-explanatory.'

'Considering your dedication to your career, this is a

trigger response you *will* regret in the very near future,' he snapped. 'I'm willing to overlook it if you are.'

'No, thank you.'

He looked askance, genuinely puzzled. 'Excuse me?'

Sienna took a moment to breathe. 'I'm not going to debate the matter with you. Thankfully, my employment, like my attire, is no longer a subject you have a say on. The copy I sent you by email was unsigned. I believe this makes it official.' She took the requisite steps forward to place the signed resignation letter on his desk before retreating to her position in the middle of the room.

He took his time to scrutinise her face, probing long and deep with penetrating eyes, before he deigned to pick up the piece of paper. After a cursory glance, he flung it back on his desk.

'I do not accept this.'

'You have very little choice in the matter, Mr Castillo,' she replied, her voice less than warm.

His jaw flexed and his nostrils flared. 'You forget that I have to approve this ridiculous "with immediate effect" resignation. And give whatever future employer you choose a worthy reference.'

'If you're under the misconceived notion that I intend to bow and scrape to remain in your good books for the sake of a so-called *worthy reference*, consider this a heads-up that it's not going to happen. I've had assurances of my pick of the top five hedge funds for the last six months should I ever choose to leave Castillo Ventures.'

His head snapped back, his mouth thinning into a line of displeasure. 'You've been courting other companies behind my back?'

Unexpected laughter scraped her throat raw. 'Please let's refrain from flinging accusations of what's happened behind whose back.'

His face tightened. 'I can still make things difficult for you. You know this.'

She deliberately relaxed her limbs, returning his gaze with contrived boredom. 'To what end, though? Besides the rank display of sour grapes on your part, I know one or two CEOs who will hire me simply to get back at you for deals you snatched from right under their noses.'

His eyelids swept down and his fingers formed a steeple on his desk, both signs that his clever brain was ticking over, finding another angle of attack. Sienna braced herself.

'The requisite notice period for someone in your position is six weeks, or have you forgotten that clause in your contract? I can compel you to stay by law.'

Her insides hollowed. 'You would have me stay, be the subject of pitied whispers and lunchtime gossip?'

Indomitable eyes locked on her. 'It only affects you if you allow it. I still maintain that what goes on between us is nobody's business,' he hissed.

Words she'd heard before, the last time whispered against her mouth in this very office, right before a kiss that had made her whole being sing. Words that now made her insides bleed. 'You're wrong, first, to imply there's an *us*. There isn't. I'm beginning to think there never was. Second, you made it everyone's business by taking out a front-page spread about your engagement to another woman!'

He jerked to his feet and rounded his desk, striding towards her. 'I didn't take out a spread. These things just happen!'

She backed away several steps, already fearing her hastily stitched-into-place façade was crumbling. 'I'm sure they do in your world. I want no part of it. I'm leaving. Let me know who you decide to pick as my successor. I'll stay for the rest of the week to bring them up to speed on my projects. I have two months' accrued vacation. If you insist on me working my notice, take that.'

'That's not how it works.'

'Too bad. Sue me if you have to, but on this subject, and on everything else not directly pertaining to Castillo Ventures business, you and I don't have anything more to say to each other, Mr Castillo.'

'Damn it, stop calling me that!' The sharp words were accompanied by a savage shove of his fingers through his hair as he eyed her from the charged space between them.

The unexpected score of needling him should've soothed the torrent of despair inside her. Instead, rough anguish only dug its talons deeper. 'I will *never* call you by your first name again,' she replied in a ragged whisper. 'If you insist on prolonging this farce, I *will* find other names for you, though.'

He shoved his fists in his pockets, his unwavering stare drilling holes into her. 'You really insist on doing this? On throwing your precious career away?'

'How arrogant of you to believe I'll only be a success with you,' she returned with a scornful glare. 'How insufferable of you to imagine I won't thrive with anyone else but you.'

He sauntered towards her with slow, measured, predatory steps. 'You think anyone else can offer you what I have, *querida*? Fire up your intellect or stimulate you the way I do?'

She stared at him, a part of her still reeling and running for cover from the events of the past twelve hours. The other traitorous part wanted to unfurl itself at the warmth of the memories he was callously evoking, to bask shamelessly in bygones.

Brutally, she superimposed her to-do list onto the memories, reminding herself that she had a purpose far away

from this man and this place. That she was worth more
than this humiliation.

'You are far from the unique gem you imagine yourself
to be, Mr Castillo. Don't worry about me. I'll be fine. I'm
looking forward to the challenge, actually. Now, if we're
done here, I think I'll take you up on that offer of a day
off. I need to go apartment hunting.'

Emotion akin to shock flashed briefly through his eyes.
'You're moving out of the penthouse?'

'Moved. Past tense.'

'Why? The papers are drawn up, Sienna. It's yours,
free and clear.'

'No, thanks. I don't want *anything* from you.'

Not entirely true. What she'd wanted, he'd cruelly made
clear would never be hers.

His eyes darkened to hard stone. A muscle ticked in his
cheek as he closed the gap between them.

'Are you quite sure, *querida*? You will not have a chance
to change your mind.'

'One hundred per cent,' she replied through clenched
teeth.

For endless seconds he stared at her while her heart
hammered a wild tattoo against her ribs. Then he jerked
his square chin at the door behind her.

'Go, then. Forget me…if you can,' he taunted.

She turned on her heel, forcing herself not to take that
one last, desperate fill of him. Her hand grasping the door
handle, she paused. Because she needed to say this, as
much for herself as for him.

'I *will* forget you. With pleasure.'

There weren't many parts of the world she could go without memories of Emiliano dogging her. But she tried, re-
warding herself the moment she left Castillo Ventures a
week later with a plane ticket to South America.

The Inca Trail to Machu Picchu served a dual purpose of being an Emiliano-free zone and a physically taxing enough trek to aid her to dreamless slumber in her tent each night.

But any numbness she'd managed to wrap herself in fled the moment she landed at Heathrow four weeks later and turned her phone back on to floods of texts and emails. Sienna forced herself to ignore them as she settled into the back of her taxi and recited her to-do list.

Unpack and settle into her new flat.

Find a job.

Find a way to stop desperately missing the man who'd cruelly rejected her.

She clenched her fist when her heart lurched in that irritatingly dramatic way it did whenever she thought of him.

She had the rest of her life to get on with. Thankfully, the taxi journey to her new address in Chelsea was short. Sienna wasn't ashamed to admit she'd chosen to live on the opposite side of the city to where Emiliano's penthouse was located in East London. She had even contemplated moving out of London altogether. Except that would mean he'd won. She still had some pride left.

Pride that wobbled when she walked into her two-bedroom flat and saw the seven meagre boxes and three suitcases that formed the sum total of her existence. She'd never felt the lack of belonging as acutely as she felt it in that moment.

Angrily, she swiped at the tears that spiked her eyes and got to work. Two hours later, new furniture ordered and boxes unpacked, she tackled her emails.

The only communication from Emiliano was via his HR department. Her severance package was exactly what she was owed and not a penny more. Sienna had insisted on it. So, subject to a few final forms to sign and return, she was officially free of Emiliano Castillo.

Ignoring another squeeze of her heart, she scrutinised the job offers the headhunter had sent. She was about to respond to the one that looked halfway appealing when her mobile phone rang.

A quick check of the screen and she was berating herself for the jolt of disappointment. Pulling herself together, she answered.

'You're back. Thank the Lord! My phone has been ringing off the hook with offers. I have... Wait for it... *Six* hedge funders dying to talk to you.'

David Hunter, the aptly named headhunter who'd made it his business to call her at least once a month for the last year in an attempt to steal her from Castillo Ventures, was as relentless as he was charming. She'd met with him briefly twice before leaving for South America. At their second meeting she hadn't failed to detect the personal interest in his eyes. The warmth in his voice now was a welcome balm to a loneliness she didn't want to admit to feeling, even though she had no intention of entertaining that interest.

'Wow,' she murmured half-heartedly.

He laughed. 'Um, maybe try that again, with feeling?'

Sienna chose to view the small smile that curved her lips as progress. 'Sorry. Jet lag.' It wasn't completely a false statement. Her twelve-hour journey and her frenzied attempt to make her flat habitable had sapped the last of her energy reserves. Her head felt heavy and she wanted to sleep for a week.

'I'll let you go if you agree to have dinner with me tomorrow to discuss the offers,' he pressed.

'I'm not sure, David. Can I let you know?'

He paused for a beat before replying, 'Okay, here's my mini pitch. You're in a unique position to choose your next job, Sienna. Everyone wants you. Castillo is a market leader, sure, but there are other equally exciting opportunities out there for you. They won't stay on the table for ever. I don't want you to miss out on them.'

The vice around her heart squeezed painfully at the mention of Castillo. And as with every time it happened, it also brought a tiny spark of anger. She couldn't mope for ever.

'Okay, dinner tomorrow.'

'Wonderful. Do you have a cuisine preference?'

She thought for a single second before she named her favourite restaurant. As with every corner of her life, it was time to root Emiliano out of this one, too.

'Great, shall I pick you up at seven?'

Because that smacked too much of a date, Sienna shook her head. 'No, it's fine. I'll meet you there.'

His response remained enthusiastic, even if his tone held a touch of disappointment. Finishing the conversation, she made herself a cup of tea and slice of toast. Half-heartedly eating her meal, she took her first shower in her new apartment, then fell into bed.

Twelve hours later, she woke, refreshed if a little listless. Finding herself with next to nothing to do in the middle of a work week was a strange sensation. On a whim, she dressed, snatched up her handbag and caught the Tube to King's Road. After buying a few practical items she needed for her flat, she splurged on a bright bouquet of flowers and a new dress.

She hated that everything in her wardrobe had an Emiliano-sized reminder tag on it, but throwing it all out and starting anew was one step too far. The new emerald silk dress was chic enough for a dinner while projecting a professional air. And, when the time came to get ready, she teamed it with black slingback shoes, black pearls and a matching bracelet. After sliding on her favourite red lipstick, she picked up her clutch and made her way outside to the waiting taxi.

Zarcosta was a Michelin-starred restaurant, which specialised in European dishes with a distinct Mediterranean flavour. The owner, Marco Zarcosta, was effusive and temperamental, a short, bespectacled character who either loved or hated clients on sight. Sienna had been lucky enough to be enfolded in the former group and she was met with a hug and a kiss on both cheeks when she entered the intimately lit restaurant in Fitzrovia.

'A shame about this relationship business, *cara*,' the Italian murmured in her ear. 'Such a shame. But Marco is here for you, eh?'

Pulling back from the embrace, she nodded and plastered on a smile, while wondering if coming here had been a wise choice. But David, having spotted her, was rising from the table and making his way towards her.

With his gelled blond hair, sparkling silver-grey eyes and a flashing smile, it wasn't a stretch to picture David Hunter as a surfer, the only thing differentiating him from that carefree lifestyle being his three-piece suit and the look of determination in his eyes. Determination that morphed to intimate interest when his eyes met hers. A quick once-over of her body and his smile widened.

'Glad you made it. You look fantastic.'

'Um, thanks.'

Although she was a little taken aback when he cupped her elbows and repeated Marco's version of kissing her hello, she wasn't altogether surprised.

What did surprise her, though, and what sent a tectonic jolt of electricity through her as she cast a gaze across the full room on her way to their table, was the sight of Emiliano Castillo staring at her with chilling eyes.

CHAPTER FOUR

SHE STUMBLED. She *actually* stumbled.

Cringing and hating herself for the telling action, she plastered an even wider smile on her face as David caught and steadied her.

'Hey, you okay?'

'Of course, why shouldn't I be?' The question emerged a touch more aggressively than she'd intended.

His eyes widened a little before he offered her a sympathetic smile. 'Sorry if I came on a little strong yesterday,' he said as he pulled out her chair and saw her seated. 'Landing you will do wonders for my account,' he said shamelessly. 'Not to mention my street cred.'

Her laugh was a little forced, her nerves screeching with horror to find that her every sense was attuned to the man across the room. The one whose piercing gaze she could feel boring into her skin.

'Well, I do need a job, so let's hear what's on the table.'

'Excellent. First, I'll order us some wine. Or would you like champagne? We might have something to celebrate at the end of the evening, I expect. You don't think I'm jumping the gun, do you?'

She gave a carefree wave of her hand. 'Not at all. Go for it,' she replied with enthusiasm that echoed patently false inside.

His smile brightened. Thankfully, he was not picking up on her act. Their waiter arrived. David ordered their drinks and she ordered her favourite meal. Simply because she wasn't about to give in to the voice mocking her about her situation.

The moment they were alone, David started raving about the offers.

She listened. She nodded. She even managed one or two pertinent questions.

But they all sounded boring. Nothing as intellectually stimulating as the work she'd done at Castillo.

You think anyone else can offer you what I have, querida?

His voice was as clear as a bell in her head. So much so, her head snapped towards the man in question. His stare was direct and unapologetic. Cold and arrogant. His dinner companions, a male and female she didn't recognise, were making conversation. He nodded and said something back. All without taking his gaze off her.

Sienna grew hot. Then cold. Hot again. As if her body didn't know what to make of the circumstances.

Warm fingers drifted over the back of her hand. 'Hey, I'm not losing you, am I?'

She started, looked down at David's hand on hers. Then absurdly, because a part of her remained a glutton for punishment, she glanced back at Emiliano.

His already-hardened face had grown tauter, his jaw clenched in steel as his gaze dropped to take in the caress. The look in his eyes when their gazes reconnected was no longer Arctic cold. It was furnace hot with censure.

She wanted to laugh but she was sure the action would strangle her. So she turned away, focused her gaze on her dinner companion and smiled.

'No, you're not losing me. In fact, I want to hear more about Chrysallis. They sound like they could be a great fit.'

Their starters arrived. She ate without tasting a morsel while David dove into his role with even more gusto, pausing only when their plates were cleared away.

Needing a breather because the weight of Emiliano's regard was unsettling her more by the minute, she placed her napkin on the table and picked up her clutch.

'Would you excuse me for a minute? I need to visit the ladies' room.'

'Of course.' He rose immediately and solicitously came round to pull back her chair. Before she could step away, he leaned down towards her. 'And I know it's a little awkward having your old boss in the same room while discussing your next job. Sorry about that.'

Startled, she turned to look at him. Sympathetic grey eyes met hers and, for some absurd reason, a lump rose in her throat. 'It's not your fault, but thank you for understanding.'

He nodded, then stood back to her let pass.

The much-needed composure gathering took five long minutes of pacing the empty ladies' room, water splashed on her hot wrists and reapplication of her lipstick. Reminding herself that she'd been through worse adversity—because what was worse than being rejected by four different foster families within the space of a year when you're eleven years old?—she squared her shoulders and pulled open the ladies' room door.

To find Emiliano leaning against the wall, feet planted in patent aggression.

The look in his eyes hadn't changed. In fact, he looked even angrier, his every breath evocative of the dark rumbling of a volcano before it erupted and destroyed everything in its path.

Sienna reminded herself that they were done. She didn't need to engage him, even though every fibre of her being insisted on straining towards him.

Forcing her gaze from his tall, sleek body, she took a step away from him.

One hand shot out to grip her waist, long fingers imprisoning her.

'You really want to play it like this? You want to pretend I don't exist?' he snarled at her.

What his deep voice did to her insides, she didn't like. Not one little bit. 'You don't exist, not to me. You challenged me to forget you, remember? This is me forgetting you.'

'By bringing another man *here*, on your first date?'

'Why, did you think this place would stop being special to me because you dumped me? Why should I stop coming here? The food is great, the ambience is excellent and the company sublime. And what makes you think it's a first date?' she threw in with a raised eyebrow.

Leonine eyes glinted pure danger. 'How many times have you seen him?'

She sighed. 'Why do you care? It really is none of your business.'

He opened his mouth then clamped it shut again when a trio of women came down the hall. His hold moved lightning quick from her waist to her wrist, taking it in an implacable hold and using it to compel her through another door. Between one moment and the next, they were outside in a quiet alley, the sound of dining guests and cutlery cut off abruptly.

'How many?' he growled again.

A dart of apprehension lanced her that had nothing to do with the cold temperature and light falling rain. But with it came a dose of something else: excitement.

She hated herself for it. He'd left her. Rejected her in the worst possible way in favour of something better. *Someone* better. Just as her mother had done. Just as all the potential foster families had done. She didn't owe him the time of day, never mind this conversation. But she would answer him. If nothing else, there was the matter of her pride. The silent treatment never worked with him. She'd learned very early in their relationship—their *ex*-relationship—that Emiliano was arrogant enough to think he'd won an argument whenever she chose silence instead of answering.

'This is our third date.' She proffered the lie coolly, keeping her gaze squarely on his. She knew what her answer would mean to him. Was morbidly curious to see the effect it had on him.

Because Emiliano never forgot.

He went marble-still, his chest barely rising and falling. Sienna knew what it meant. She'd struck a very raw nerve. Part of her rejoiced. Even as a greater part of her curled up and died for that rejoicing. Because what did that say about her? That she was so hung up on him, she wanted to get a rise out of him for delivering information that was sure to remind him of them? That would remind him that they'd made love for the first time after their third date?

'Your *third* date?' he repeated ominously.

She raised her chin, shivering despite the volcanic atmosphere between them.

He spotted her reaction and started to shrug off his jacket, the way he'd done numerous times in the past when she'd needed an extra layer of warmth.

She stepped back quickly, unable to bear the thought. 'What do you think you're doing?'

He paused. 'You need to ask?'

She shook her head emphatically. 'No, thank you.'

Jaw clenched, he shouldered the jacket back on, his frown turning blacker. 'Answer me, Sienna.'

'Yes, *third* date. And it's going very well, even if I say so myself. I've just ordered the oysters. If you haven't had your main yet, I suggest you try them. Marco's outdoing himself tonight.'

He took a single, predatory step towards her, his face a mask of frozen fury. 'Who is he, Sienna, hmm? This guy you're eating oysters for?'

She affected what she hoped was a half-decent indifferent shrug. 'He's the guy who may or may not know what the significance of a third date with me means. He's witty, charming and intelligent, and we have oodles in common, so I'd say his prospects are—'

The single, filthy curse was her only warning before Emiliano grabbed her by the arms and slammed her against the wall. To anyone witnessing the action, it might have seemed violent, but it was a practised move perfected in their time together that ensured her no harm. The reminder sent everything inside Sienna screaming with mingled horror and sheer delight as electricity rushed through her. It was the most natural response in the world to start raising one leg in preparation to have him hitching her up. But the assist never came. And in the dark alley, the cold wind reminded her that it was over between Emiliano and her.

That this conversation should not be happening.

'You will *not* sleep with him,' he pronounced darkly, his thinned lips white with restrained fury.

She laughed. It was either that or succumb to something else—such as tears. 'Do you need a reminder of how I react to orders, Mr Castillo?'

His face tightened further at her deliberate formality. 'Unless you were seeing him behind my back, you barely know the guy. For all you know he could be—'

'What? Someone else who leads me along for over a year then dumps me for his fiancée?'

He had the grace to drop his gaze, to blink, but it was the only give in an otherwise rigidly unforgiving but breathtakingly striking face.

'Sienna, things aren't what they seem. I told you why I'm doing this—'

'Let me go. Go finish your meeting. Then go home to your fiancée. I'm not sure exactly what you intended by cornering me this way. But if somewhere in your twisted imagination you thought you were looking out for me, then don't. We both know I've never been the feeble, cuddly type. You hurt me, but as you can see I didn't curl up and die. I don't intend to. I've moved on.'

She placed her hands on his chest and pushed. For a moment, he didn't budge. Then he stepped back. Sienna wished he'd stayed a moment longer. And cursed herself to hell and back.

She moved from the wall and ran damp hands over her dress. When she raised her head, he was regarding her with icy mockery.

'I thought you many things, but I never thought the day would come when I'd think you a petty fool.'

Her mouth dropped open. 'Excuse me?'

He shrugged. 'Deny it if you will, that all of this was staged for my benefit. You didn't hope I would see you with another man and immediately come running back?'

She forced her mouth closed and raised a hand casually to flick her long hair over her shoulder. A sliver of satisfaction came with witnessing the trace of hunger on his face as he followed the movement.

'You have a particular word in Argentina for a donkey's behind, don't you, Mr Castillo? I'm sure I heard you use it once or twice, usually when things weren't going your way. Well, guess what? You're being a giant one right now.' She stepped close, even though her every instinct screamed at her to flee in the other direction, and she continued, 'The only thing I want you thinking about me tonight, when you get home and are enjoying your favourite cognac, is how much I appreciate everything you taught me in bed during our time together. And how much I'm going to be enjoying sharing all that gorgeous, decadent knowledge with David. And then I want you to raise that glass to yourself, because you truly deserve the kudos—'

'*Cállate!*' Grasping her arms, he pinned her back against the wall, a feverish light glinting dangerously in his eyes. 'Shut the hell up!' he repeated in English. With each snarled word, he moved her higher up the wall until he was eye level with her. 'You want a reaction from me, *enamorada*? Well, your wish is about to be granted.'

The kiss was hell. And heaven. And everything in between. The edgy hunger and fury with which Emiliano kissed her, devoured her, robbed her of thought in a single second. All she could feel, breathe, hear, was the riotous, ecstatic thundering of her senses.

With a helpless groan, she opened her mouth and welcomed a kiss that should not have been happening. Whether it was the illicit nature of it or, because contrary to what she'd been telling herself he continued to be vital to her very being, Sienna was too afraid to find out. All she could stand to entertain in that moment was that he was here for a brief moment in her arms. The man who had taught her the finest art of passion was in her arms. And she didn't want to let him go.

His moan echoed hers as the kiss deepened, their strained panting echoing in the dark alley as the rain intensified, hands roving, touch reacquainted. Her hands slid over his shoulders, locked into the vibrant hair at his nape and scraped over his scalp.

He jerked against her, the imprint of his powerful arousal a primal force at the cradle of her thighs. She couldn't help it, she moved against him, her tongue sliding sensuously against his in blatant, desperate need as her body melted. He shifted, placing a little distance between them.

Sienna whimpered and started to close the gap. Felt the mist of rain on her face. Then it all came rushing back.

Emiliano stepped away, eyes blazing but face frozen once more.

'Go now, *querida*. Return to your *date* with my touch all over your body. Go to him and tell him I was the one who made you wet, who caused that glazed look in your eyes and your swollen lips. Tell him how I could've had you right here, right now, against this wall if I wished. And if he wants you after that—' he shrugged '—try telling yourself he's still the charming and intelligent man you want.'

Anger swiftly followed shock and shame. 'You…you're disgusting. I hate you!'

'Be truthful. You don't hate me. You hate yourself because your little game has been turned back on you.'

Thick, gulping tears threatened. Sienna battled them back through sheer grit. But even after she got herself under a modicum of control she couldn't speak. She stared at him, the man she'd allowed to mean more to her in their time together than had been even remotely wise. She'd paid heavily for that gross misjudgement. Was still paying. As she gazed into his powerfully gorgeous face, she shook her head.

'You're right. I don't hate you. What I feel is sadness for you—that you feel the need to do this just to prove a point. But I don't hate myself for trying to move on. You can do your best to belittle my efforts—it's not going to stop me. You can either move on, too, or waste your time trying to corner me in dark alleys. No matter what you do or say or try to prove, all you'll get is me, walking away from you every time.'

A cryptic expression washed over his face, followed by another, before his mask slipped back into place. 'Great speech, *querida*, but perhaps if you'd stop for a minute you can hear what I have to say.'

'I don't want to hear it. You and I had nothing to talk about when I left you last month. We have even less to talk about now.'

He lifted a lazy hand and passed a finger over her tingling lower lip. 'Our kiss said otherwise.'

She jerked away. 'The kiss I'm already incredibly ashamed of, you mean?'

His face darkened and his hand dropped. 'Excuse me?'

'You're not deaf. You're engaged to another woman, and yet here you are, kissing me. Don't you have even a shred of decency?'

He shook his head. 'Sienna, it's not going to be like that—'

'No! Enough. And stop saying my name,' she snapped. Prying herself off the wall, she started walking away.

'Come back here,' he bit out. 'We're not finished.'

She hurried her steps, almost fearful her feet would disobey her and rush back to him, to hear him out if it meant hearing his voice, seeing his face for a few more precious minutes. She heard him behind her and quickened her steps.

'*Dios mío*, stop!'

She broke into a run, catching a sob before it slipped free.

'Sienna, slow down!'

She saw a mound of snow swept to one side of the pavement, she heard voices from pedestrians at the entrance to the alley and ran faster. The urgency to get back to civility, away from Emiliano's captivating presence, rushed through her. What had she been thinking? He belonged to another woman. He was no longer hers to kiss, to touch, to make love with...

The sob broke, horrible and pain-filled. Tears surged into her eyes, blinding her. She rounded the corner at full speed. She never knew whether it was a body or an object she bumped into. But she felt her heel slide over the icy sidewalk. Felt her body wrenched sideways as she lost her balance. Saw the ground rush up to meet her. Heard Emiliano's guttural shout from behind. Then felt excruciating pain as her head cracked on the side of the kerb, her braced arms doing nothing to halt her fall.

She moaned as stars exploded across her vision. Hands turned her, cradled her. Her vision cleared for a second and she saw golden eyes filled with concern blazing down at her. Then another rip of pain.

Then the blissful succumbing to nothing.

CHAPTER FIVE

'MISS NEWMAN? SIENNA?'

She turned her head a fraction towards the sound but kept her eyes closed. The effort it took to move even her eyeballs was too much.

'Hmm…?'

'Don't try and speak, Miss Newman. Take it easy. Open your eyes when you're ready.'

Miss Newman? Was there someone else in the room with her? Was the voice speaking to someone else besides her? She would much prefer it because having someone engage with her would mean she had to respond. She would have to speak. She turned away from the voice. She didn't want to speak. She wanted to sink back into the harmless abyss where there was no pain, only oblivion. Where there were no voices murmuring, drawing closer to where she lay.

'We need to take your vitals, find out how you're doing. You've been out for a while.'

Out? Where?

She tried to turn her head again, felt the restriction across her forehead and paused. She was wearing some sort of a cap. Tentatively, she lifted her hand to her head.

'That's your bandage. It needs to stay on for a while, I'm afraid,' a kind female voice supplied. 'Can you open your eyes for me, dear? The doctor needs to examine you properly.'

Doctor. She was in a hospital. But… Why?

Dropping her hand back onto her stomach, she carefully cracked her eyes open, then winced at the bright lights overhead.

'Nurse, turn down the lights, please?'

The lights dimmed. She opened her eyes a little wider.

Two faces stared at her. The male doctor wore glasses behind which dark eyes gleamed with serious intelligence. The nurse's face was kinder, more maternal.

She smiled broadly now, almost as if her patient opening her eyes was a personal triumph for her.

'I'm Dr Stephens, this is Nurse Abby. Can you tell me the last thing you remember, Miss Newman?'

She brought her attention back to the doctor. She blinked tired eyes again, casting a look around the room to make sure he was talking to someone else and not her.

He couldn't be addressing her.

Because she wasn't Miss Newman. Or Sienna.

Her name was…

It was…

She shook her head, trying to clear her brain of the thick fog.

'I…' she croaked. Her throat was raw and painful. Her voice felt disused. Raising her hand to her throat, she massaged her skin, then froze when she saw the needle inserted into her vein. Examining the back of her hand closely, she saw several puncture marks. For some reason, the sight of the tiny bruises struck fear into her heart. Her eyes sought the health professionals staring down at her. 'I… How long…?'

Dr Stephens scribbled on a sheet before he pulled out a pen light. 'You've been unconscious for a little over two weeks. The bandage on your head is because we had to perform a minor surgery to reduce the swelling on your brain.'

'Brain…*surgery*?'

'Yes.' He stepped up to the bed and held up the light, the question clear in his eyes. When she gave a small nod, he shone it in one eye, then the other. Then he stepped back. 'Can you tell me the last thing you remember?' he asked again.

A series of fragmented images flashed through her brain, like strobe lights in a dark room, on and off, before she could form a proper picture. Shaking her head again, she tried to concentrate, to capture one solid image. Her mind remained a dark, blank space.

She saw the doctor and nurse exchange glances.

'Please…' She stopped when her throat protested. The nurse stepped forward with a glass of water and straw. Gratefully, she sipped, relief pouring through her when the pain eased. 'What's… What happened?' she managed. 'Where am I?'

'You're at North Haven,' Dr Stephens replied. 'We're a private medical facility just outside London. As for what happened, you slipped on ice outside a restaurant and hit your head hard enough to cause a little brain bleed. You don't remember?'

She shook her head. 'No.'

'Do you remember going to the restaurant?' He stopped and checked his notes. 'I believe it's called Zarcosta?'

Again she shook her head, fighting the surge of panic. 'I don't…remember.'

The doctor fell silent for almost a minute, his professional mask slipping briefly to exhibit his concern. 'Miss Newman, can you tell me your date of birth?' he pressed gently.

She probed her mind desperately, and found only black space. Her throat clogged. She swallowed, refusing to succumb to tears. 'No,' she whispered. 'Is that my name— Newman? Sienna Newman?'

Dr Stephens nodded solemnly. 'Yes, it is. Do you know what you do for a living? Or where you live?'

'I don't know!' This time she couldn't stop the rise of

tears or the twisting of her hand into the sheet for something, anything, to hang on to. 'Why can't I remember?'

'I can't give you an answer yet. Not until we run a few tests.' He put away his pen light and attempted a smile. 'Try not to worry. We'll know what's going on very shortly.'

He turned and spoke to the nurse in medical jargon she couldn't decipher.

She looked down. Her hands were trembling. In fact, her whole body was trembling as confusion and panic rose in steady waves.

Sensing her emotions, Nurse Abby patted her hand. 'The technicians and I will run the tests the doctor needs, then we'll take it from there, okay?'

She couldn't do much else but nod and watch with climbing despair as they left the room. Then, forcing herself to calm down, she probed her mind again, searching every corner until tears spilled down her cheeks and exhaustion weighed her down.

She could barely summon the energy to take interest in what was happening when the nurse returned with two other medical staff. Blood was taken and her vitals recorded before she was wheeled away and placed in an MRI machine.

Time passed. Then she was returned to her room, by which time oblivion was a welcome relief. So she gave in. The sunlight outside her window had turned to night when she woke up. Her room was bathed in soft light and a breathtaking bouquet of flowers—calla lilies and white roses—stood on the dresser across the room.

The pain in her head still throbbed but she was getting used to it, enough to be able to recall the conversation with the medical team.

Even though a practical voice prompted her that panicking would bring no answers, she couldn't stop the fear squeezing her heart.

She'd had brain surgery. And now she couldn't remember her own name.

She was still grappling with the million questions teeming in her mind when Nurse Abby walked back in.

'Have I... Have there been any visitors? My family?' she blurted, the question seeming to come from nowhere.

The nurse cast a furtive glance at her before busying herself with checking the intravenous drip. 'We weren't given details of any family members to contact, but we called your...' She paused, unnecessarily straightening the sheets. 'Your friend. He's on his way.'

'My friend?' she repeated, hope momentarily robbing her of breath.

'Yes. He says he was with you that night. You're very lucky to have him. He's been here every day since your accident. He's had a bunch of those lovely flowers delivered every day, too,' she said, with a trace of envy in her voice.

Sienna—the name was still so alien to her—returned her gaze to the flowers. They were her favourite. She didn't understand how she knew, but the knowledge wasn't one that needed probing. That tiny revelation of self eased the panic threatening again. Not enough to keep her from going on a desperate hunt for her memory once again, though, and experiencing the hollowness in her stomach expand when she found nothing. Retreating from her mental flailing, she latched on to the only real thing available.

'My friend... What's his name?' she asked.

'It's... Oh, here he is now! We have our share of celebrities using this facility, but none of them arrive by helicopter,' she divulged in an excited whisper as she peered out of the window.

Although Sienna couldn't see the spectacle capturing the nurse's attention, she heard the distinct beating of rotor blades, the sound growing louder as the aircraft flew overhead.

As she absorbed the news that she had a friend who owned a helicopter, a buzzer sounded in the room. Nurse Abby dragged her attention from the window, reached into her pocket and withdrew a miniature tablet.

'Perfect timing. Your test results are ready. Dr Stephens will want to see them before he talks to you both.'

'Both?'

Nurse Abby paused by the door. 'I'm not one to gossip, but your man isn't the kind to take no for an answer. He's demanded to know every detail of your progress. And, with us not being able to contact any family members, we've had to rely on him to give medical approval. Which is a good thing, because his consent saved your life. It's clear he cares a great deal about you.' Again, Sienna caught wistfulness in her tone that told her Nurse Abby was a romantic at heart.

'So he knows I have a...um...memory issue?'

The older woman's face softened in sympathy. 'Don't worry about that, my dear. Everything will be all right. I just know it.'

Her tablet buzzed again. She was gone before Sienna could voice any of the questions burning on her tongue. And for the next twenty minutes they grew until she heard voices approaching.

Dr Stephens entered, a file in his hand. Paralysed with fear as to what that file contained and what her diagnosis was, she didn't immediately acknowledge the other presence in the room, not until she felt the tingle from the power of his stare. Not until her heart began to flutter wildly, from reasons that had nothing to do with the sorry state of her mind.

Her reaction to the man partly obscured by Dr Stephens's advancing form was so visceral, so primitively electrifying, her fingers locked on to the sheets and her breath strangled in her throat.

'Miss Newman, I have the results of your tests. Before
we continue, Nurse Abby informs me she's told you of Mr
Castillo's involvement in your medical care.' He rounded
to the side of the bed, stepping out of the line of sight of
the man behind him. The man who stood tall, imposing.
Frozen at the sight of her. 'You won't remember him, most
likely, but this is…'

The buzzing in her ears stopped her from hearing the
rest of Dr Stephen's words.

From the tiny pieces of useless, broken memory, a single
one began to form. Not a whole picture, but enough frac-
tions coalesced to make her heart skip several beats. To
make her whole body tremble into wakeful, joyful aware-
ness when the piece held.

Enough to make her stare at the man whose face, like a
blazing comet through the night sky, was beautifully real
and infinitely magical to her.

'Emiliano…' Her voice emerged as a hopeful rasp.
When he didn't disappear, when he remained a solid, tow-
ering reality before her, she struggled upright. 'Emiliano!'

He took a single step towards her then froze again, his
face losing several shades of colour. 'You remember?' he
rasped, a peculiar note in his voice as he stared with watchful, almost-alarmed eyes.

'Yes! I remember you. Oh, God!' Her gaze darted ex-
citedly to the doctor and back to Emiliano. 'I remember!'

He still hadn't moved. Why? Did she look that horrific? She knew from the brief and cringe-making self-
examination she'd conducted earlier that she'd lost weight.
There were hollows not just on the inside of her but also
on the outside.

But Emiliano had nursed her through a horrific flu and
chest infection recently without batting an eyelash. And
she was sure she'd looked worse then.

Realising she'd just had another memory, she gasped. 'The flu! I had the flu around a month ago,' she said.

Dr Stephens glanced at Emiliano. His jaw flexed for a second before he shook his head and they both stared at her.

'What?' she demanded.

'Your flu wasn't a month ago. It was in late September.'

'And?'

'And it'll be New Year's Day in three days,' he said, his deep voice curiously flat.

Her heart lurched, then thudded anew with dread. Before it could take complete hold, Dr Stephens cleared his throat.

'Miss Newman, can you tell me what your relationship is with Mr Castillo?'

She glanced at Emiliano, her panic receding a little as his eyes met hers. 'We're lovers,' she said, blushing when his eyes began to darken. The word *lover* had always felt a little too intimate to share, but she couldn't think of a better term to describe the relationship between her and Emiliano. 'We've been together for nearly ten months.'

A rough sound emerged from his throat. He must be worried about her. He hadn't liked it when she'd got her chest infection. She couldn't imagine what the last two weeks had been like for him. In a reversed position, she would've been out of her mind.

Tentatively, she reached out her unencumbered hand to him. 'Emiliano, I'm okay. I'm sorry if I worried you.'

After a tense little moment, he moved towards her. The hand that enfolded hers was warm, strong. Stimulatingly electrifying. Her breath caught all over again when she raised her head and saw their touch was having the same effect on him.

They both turned when Dr Stephens cleared his throat again. 'Mr Castillo, can you corroborate that?'

'No. It's been longer than that. About a year, to be exact,' he said.

'A *year*?' She searched his eyes.

'*Si,*' he confirmed.

Thrown into confusion all over again, she struggled to breathe. 'What's wrong with me?'

'You're showing all the signs of retrograde amnesia,' Dr Stephens said. 'Your head trauma has caused you to lose chunks of your memory. Can you tell me your earliest memory of you and Mr Castillo?'

She frowned, sifted through the jagged pieces. 'I… We were in Vienna…at the summer opera…in June?' She glanced up at Emiliano. He nodded.

'And the last?' the doctor asked.

'Um… It must be October, then. A client meeting in Vancouver, followed by dinner. I was feeling much better by then.' She couldn't stop the flow of colour into her cheeks as other memories burst forth. The tightening of his hand on hers told her he was recalling the hastily made excuses after the deal had been struck, the abandoned meal, the frenzied kiss in the lift, Emiliano lapping vintage champagne from her naked body.

He'd murmured thick, charged words to her in Spanish as he'd made love to her. Words she was beginning to understand. Words that had sparked the belief that she wasn't just another transient body, warming his bed for a finite spell.

'So you remember what you do for a living now?'

She nodded. 'I'm his… I'm the vice-president of Acquisitions at Castillo Ventures.'

Dr Stephens's gaze flicked to Emiliano before it returned to her. 'Anything else? Your age? Family? Favourite soccer team?'

She held her breath and delved deep once more, her hand grasping Emiliano's tighter as she came up empty.

Swallowing, she shook her head. 'No, but I know Emiliano's birthday is in September.'

The doctor nodded. 'Okay. Let's move on to other things—'

'Wait. What… When will I get my memories back? Is there anything I can do?'

Beside her, Emiliano shifted, his free hand sliding over her nape to gently direct her gaze to him. 'Dr Stephens stresses the importance of not forcing your memories to return, *querida*. Isn't that right, doctor?'

There was something in his voice. The bone-deep authority stamped into each word and deed was nothing new to her refreshed memory, but there was underlying terseness in there.

Dr Stephens nodded. 'It's better to let the memories return on their own. Unfortunately, there isn't a time frame of when that'll be. Your brain is still healing itself after the trauma. My recommendation is for the complete absence of stress of any kind, especially considering your other condition.'

She felt Emiliano tense as her own anxiety spiked. A quick glance at him showed his darkly questioning stare levelled at the doctor. 'My other condition?' she asked.

'You said she was healing,' Emiliano accused icily.

'She is. I don't mean that.' His gaze returned to her. 'Since the time frame of your relationship is right, I'm going to assume it's okay to share this information with Mr Castillo, as well.'

'What information?' she demanded.

Dr Stephens consulted the file one last time, then closed it. 'The result of the blood test we took when you were first admitted two weeks ago revealed you are pregnant.'

Her heart somersaulted into her stomach. 'I'm… *What?*'

The hand on her nape had tightened almost to the point

of discomfort, but she didn't mind too much. It was the only thing keeping her grounded.

'Yes, doctor. Repeat that, *por favor*,' Emiliano commanded through clenched teeth.

'Obviously with the gap in her memory we won't be able to determine how far along she is, but the scan shows she can't be more than three-months pregnant.'

'How is that possible? She never missed taking her pill.'

'And you? Did you use protection?'

Emiliano replied without embarrassment. 'No. We preferred it that way. We both got blood tests to prove we were healthy.'

'She mentioned the flu and an infection. Did she take a course of antibiotics?'

Emiliano nodded tersely. 'Yes, but she got her period after that. She's as regular as clockwork.'

'But the effectiveness of the pill may have been compromised by the antibiotics. It only needed to be disrupted briefly for pregnancy to occur. And menstruating in the first month of pregnancy isn't uncommon.'

Dr Stephens carried on speaking. Emiliano fired more questions at him.

'Is the baby okay?' she asked when a lull came in the interrogation.

'Yes, we've been monitoring you closely and, besides the head injury, your body is thriving.'

Sienna exhaled in relief and turned her hand within Emiliano's, needing even more of his touch as her senses went into complete free fall. First came shock, then panic. Then…utter elation. Something in her heart, an emotion she didn't completely understand, cracked wide open, spewing endless joy through her at the thought of the baby growing inside her.

But all she could do was stare at her lover, her insides singing with happiness.

'Emiliano...' she murmured softly, a tiny part of her afraid that, like her absent memories, her new joy would disappear if she spoke too loudly.

He heard her and stopped speaking to stare down at her. His deep shock was clear in his eyes. As was a tumble of other unfathomable emotions. Emotions she was confident they would work through eventually.

'Yes, Sienna?'

'Emiliano...I'm... We're having a baby,' she whispered in wonder.

His eyes blazed with a fierce light that turned her insides molten. His gaze left hers to track down her body. It paused at her still-flat stomach and stayed, the stamp of possession unmistakeable.

His eyelids descended, temporarily veiling his expression. '*Sí, querida.* It seems we are to be unexpectedly blessed.'

Turning her head, she raised their joined hands and on impulse kissed the back of Emiliano's hand before resting her cheek against it. She heard his sharp inhalation but she refused to be embarrassed about the public display of affection.

Silence reigned for a handful of seconds before Emiliano eased away.

'Rest now. I need to speak to Dr Stephens about when you can be discharged.'

She settled back into bed, her mouth curving in a smile. 'Oh, yes, please. I can't wait to go home. Alfie must be bored out of his mind with just you for company,' she teased.

He didn't return her smile. But her instinct told her that wasn't new. 'He wouldn't dare admit it to me, but I have a feeling he will be pleased to have you back,' he offered dryly. Then he walked out.

Despite the huge obstacles she was sure awaited her

future, Sienna couldn't stop her smile stretching wide as her hand drifted down to rest on her stomach.

Some of her memories might have been temporarily taken away, but while she waited for time to heal her she would revel in what she knew in her heart was a true blessing.

CHAPTER SIX

'YOU'VE KNOWN SHE was pregnant for two weeks and you didn't tell me?' Emiliano demanded the moment the doctor shut the door behind them. He wasn't sure why his blood was boiling so high. Nor did he welcome it. The shock he'd just sustained needed to be treated with cold, calculated precision. Not this frantic pacing and hammering heartbeats.

Sienna was pregnant. The woman who he had very little doubt hated the very ground he walked on was carrying his child. The same woman who'd told him coldly two weeks ago that she'd moved on from him, and who'd blatantly flaunted another man in his face.

His gut clenched hard, the punch of that statement nowhere near dulled despite the passage of time.

The situation with the Cabreras was nowhere near resolved, despite his best efforts to find a solution. They were intent on the son paying for the sins of the parents. And they were wealthy enough not to be influenced by the offer of financial compensation.

Only Emiliano's agreement to wed Graciela Cabrera had sufficed. He'd gone along with it, thinking he would find a quick alternative solution while they were temporarily appeased.

Emiliano would've consigned the whole situation to hell by now had it not been for Matias's plea at the end of his video message and his own meeting with Graciela.

It was clear the young girl was desperate to find a way out from beneath her father's oppressive thumb, her wild behaviour and risqué media courting simply outbursts of a cornered, bewildered victim. Emiliano wasn't ashamed to admit empathy had forced him to stay at the dinner that had been photographed by the paparazzi.

Even then, he'd been all set to walk away. Despite his brother's entreaty, he'd known he needed to find another way to honour Matias's wishes. Until Graciela's blatant plea for help, for him to go along with the ruse for a short time just to buy her some time. His agreement in that moment had been to buy *himself* more time.

What he hadn't expected was for the whole situation to blow up in his face even before his feet had touched the ground properly. In light of Sienna's accident, a different powder keg had been activated, a situation that needed to be dealt with very carefully.

As for the news that he was to be a father...

He pushed that to the bottom of the list. He was pragmatic enough to accept that, whether he liked it or not, this was his new reality. Sifting through his feelings to find the correct descriptive right now would serve no useful purpose.

Neither would dwelling on the fact that this was the last thing he would've wished for, given the choice.

His question, however, needed answering. He focused on the doctor, who shrugged. 'You're not my patient. She is. I shared those details that were pertinent to her continued health with you because I needed your consent to treat her head trauma. Her pregnancy didn't fall into that purview.'

'It wasn't up to you to decide what to share and what to withhold. I'm the father of her child!' The words felt alien and almost...alarming coming from his mouth. What did he know about parenting? His own experience had been beyond abysmal to the point of non-existent.

The thought triggered a deep unsettling inside him and he had to tighten his gut against letting it rule him.

'The history you gave me when she was admitted left

room for questions. I had to do whatever I could to treat her trauma, but I couldn't share confidential information with you, because you'd told me you two were no longer together. I had to consider the possibility that someone else was the father.'

A part of him understood the doctor's reasoning. A greater part of him raged maniacally at the thought of Sienna sleeping with another man, never mind taking his seed into her body and carrying his child. He'd seen her on a date with David Hunter and he hadn't reacted well. In fact, he'd go as far as to say he'd been ashamed of himself for the way he acted. That didn't diminish his rage. Or the guilt dogging him.

Telling himself his possessive instincts had spiked and remained fiercely active when she'd walked away from him was true enough. He hadn't been anywhere near ready to let Sienna go despite his growing misgivings about her. Having the decision taken out of his hands while he'd been in retreat and regroup mode had stung.

None of that changed the fact that he was the reason she was laid up in a hospital bed with gaps in her memory. Gaps he couldn't fill without causing further damage. To her or the child.

His child.

His responsibility.

Again he experienced a bolt of bewilderment and shook his head, everything that had happened recently making him ball his fists in silent fury.

'Give me the raw prognosis. And a way forward that enables me to come clean with her about our relationship.' He abhorred the thought of lying to her.

Dr Stephens shook his head. 'My recommendation still stands. Any further trauma, even emotionally, could have a severe adverse effect on her health. Remember, it's not just her in the picture now. If she's going ahead with the pregnancy—'

'*If?*' Icy waves of disbelief washed through him, followed closely by a total rejection of the very idea. 'Why would she not want the baby?'

The other man shrugged. 'She's an independent woman, who from all accounts seems to be blocking out the last few weeks of your relationship and the break-up. You need to prepare yourself for every possibility once her memories return.'

The stark words kicked him square in the solar plexus, rocking him back on his heels.

Normally, Emiliano prided himself on seeing every angle of a problem. Spotting an opponent's strategy, being half a dozen moves ahead, picking at the flaws and beating them at their own game had seen him walk away with life-changing deals before he'd turned thirty. At thirty-two, he'd made himself, and every single one of his elite clients, unimaginably rich in the process.

But it seemed, the moment he'd set foot back in Argentina, everything had gone wrong. He'd thought himself immune to anything to do with his parents. But, when it'd come down to it, he hadn't been able to walk away. Especially not when Matias had pleaded with him on their behalf. But hard on the heels of Matias's plea on behalf of Graciela had come words which had made it impossible for him to walk away.

You owe me. And I'm collecting.

Those six words had ultimately stopped him from walking out.

He'd lost his touch. He'd lost his woman.

Now, he was faced with the very real possibility that he might lose his child. Unbidden, the scene in the alleyway played through his mind. While he'd been grappling with the increasingly demanding Cabreras and his parents, Sienna had been busy moving on, *dating* another man.

Another man she might well go back to when her memory returned. Only now she would be walking away with something that was rightfully his.

Unlike the bewildering confusion surrounding his impending fatherhood a handful of minutes ago, his thoughts were crystal clear now.

His child would be going nowhere. He might not have the first clue about how to be a parent, but neither was he prepared to take a back seat in his child's life the way his own father had done with him.

Setting his jaw, he stared at the doctor. 'When can Sienna be safely discharged?'

'I'd like to monitor her for twenty-four hours, make sure there are no setbacks.'

'And after that? What does she need to ensure she and the baby remain healthy?'

'Complete rest for a few weeks, then she can resume normal activities as long as she doesn't overdo things. I'll make sure you have a detailed aftercare programme.'

The urge to pace once again attacked him. Glancing at his watch, he realised the late hour and forced himself to curb the rest of the questions firing through his brain. 'I'll be back to collect her tomorrow. In the meantime, if she so much as twitches in discomfort—'

'You'll be my first call,' Dr Stephen finished wryly.

His walk back to Sienna's private room was a little less agitated than when he'd made the last journey. Hell, he wasn't ashamed to say that, even with this unexpected news, the vice tightening his chest had eased.

Regardless of the unwelcome emotions she'd triggered in him by attempting to walk away, *again*, from him that night, watching her fall and injure herself had been an experience he never wanted to repeat.

Knowing now that she'd taken a fall while carrying his child...

Emiliano paused outside her door, clamped a hand that was less than steady and breathed deep.

Possessiveness of the things he valued was a trait he'd recognised and shamelessly embraced very early on in his life. He hadn't needed a psychologist to tell him it was a result of having been patently *valueless* to his parents that had driven him to surround himself with material things, even sycophants, in his early adulthood. It had brought him a modicum of satisfaction, hell even a sense of belonging after long years of having been placed on a shelf and consigned to second-best status. In later years, he'd grown very selective of the things he placed value on.

Loyalty and hard work from his employees.

The growing closeness between Matias and him.

A woman in his bed who knew the score and would quietly exit his life when her time was up.

Nowhere on that list of desirable possessions had there featured a child. Not for the foreseeable future, if ever. Simply because he didn't have the right tools to forge a father-son bond.

And yet it was all he could think about now as he raised his hand and pushed the door to Sienna's room open. In the space of an hour within which the news of his impending child had been placed before him, then immediately potentially threatened, all Emiliano could think about was how to protect it. *Possess* it.

The voice that warned him against making so bold and intractable a claim was ruthlessly suppressed.

His brain working a mile a minute, he entered and crossed to the bed.

She was asleep, her long lashes fanned out against her skin. Her complexion was paler than he was used to, but she was no less breathtaking now than she'd been the first time he'd seen her across the interview table at Castillo Ventures. Now, as then, the sight of her elicited a powerful response in him, the majority of which was sexual, he admitted. But there had always been something else, something *more*, to his relationship with Sienna.

He'd never liked puzzles. His area of expertise was strategizing. Somewhere along the line he'd satisfied himself with the sound rationalisation that he would've parted ways with Sienna once he'd solved the puzzle of why she triggered this unknown…*craving* within him.

That was before other factors had stepped in and brought things to an unsatisfactory conclusion.

They'd had unfinished business before her accident.

Now they had something…different altogether.

'Emiliano?'

His gut clenched at the sound of her voice. Mere weeks ago, she'd sworn never to say his name again. Hearing it brought a peculiar sensation he couldn't quite name. Whatever it was, it wasn't enough for him not to crave hearing it again.

'*Si*, I'm here.' And he intended to be here for the foreseeable future. For the sake of the child he hadn't known existed but now could not put out of his mind.

She raised her head a fraction off the bed, the silky black hair not restricted by the bandage sliding on the pillow. 'Are you… Is everything okay?'

He drew closer, reached out and caressed her cheek. The gesture soothed her, which was supposed to be his aim, helping her remain stress-free. But he couldn't deny that he really liked touching her. 'Everything's fine. Sleep now, *querida*.'

She smiled drowsily and turned into the caress. 'I love it when you call me that.'

He tensed. He needed to stop calling her that. The endearment had slipped out without thought. But it seemed breaking habits when it came to Sienna wasn't as easy as he'd imagined.

For one thing, he'd yet to fill the position she'd vacated at Castillo Ventures. In the weeks after she'd resigned, he'd sat in on interview after interview, discarding one application after another, until one of his subordinates had suggested that perhaps the void left by Sienna was immutable.

Emiliano had snarled his disagreement. Then cancelled all following interviews.

Now his brain ticked over. Perhaps he'd been wise to keep the position open. He would have to proceed very carefully because this game could only have one outcome.

But that didn't mean he couldn't arm himself with as much ammunition in his arsenal as possible.

Whether that included leaning down to brush his lips against the cheek of the woman who subconsciously hated him was a thought he wasn't content to dwell on.

At all.

What he did concentrate on was having Sienna's belongings relocated back to the penthouse as soon as possible. The moment that task had been achieved, he called North Haven. By early evening the next day, he was landing his helicopter on the extensive lawn of the private hospital.

Discharge papers were produced, which he signed, along with a very large, very gratefully received cheque. Emiliano knew he was buying expediency, which was gratifyingly supplied. Within half an hour of landing, Sienna was being wheeled out, her suitcase carried by a porter.

Her bandage had been removed, the two-inch patch of skin where her operation had been performed replaced with a plaster and half-disguised by her long, loose hair. The shapeless hospital gown had been replaced with a cashmere jumper dress, the navy blue colour highlighting her stunning green eyes.

Eyes that now smiled at the staff who'd lined up to say goodbye.

Emiliano watched, hiding his impatience as she took the time to thank the nurses on duty before handing Nurse Abby her calla lilies and promising to stay in touch.

When she requested yet another stop to thank yet another member of staff, he put his foot down and steered her to the lift.

'No more stops. We're leaving before you wear yourself out.'

'I'm being wheeled around in the Rolls Royce of wheelchairs. I'm fine,' she replied, a grin tugging at her mouth.

Emiliano dragged his gaze away from the appealing fullness of her curved lips and stabbed at the call button. 'You've been in a coma for two weeks. Save the meet-and-greet for when you're stronger.'

She gave a mock salute. A feeble one. 'Yes, boss. Anything you say,' she said, her voice turning smoky and husky as she cast him a glance from beneath her lashes.

His gut clenched hard as he fought his libido's eager response. The last time she'd used that term, he'd bent her over his desk and showed her in no uncertain terms who was boss.

The blush staining her cheeks suggested she recalled the incident, too. The lift arrived. He stooped low to mutter in her ear as he wheeled her in, 'Behave yourself, we have an audience.'

He caught her tiny shiver before her gaze slid to the porter trailing them. It would've been an easy job to take the suitcase and dismiss him but Emiliano welcomed the buffer. It would stop him from smoothing her hair back behind her ear or leaning in to inhale her perfume.

Somewhere in the middle of the night, when he'd been polishing the finer details of his plot, he'd concluded that physical distance was crucial in order to make this madness they were embroiled in bearable. He could provide what Sienna needed without further compromising himself. Or her.

She might be forming new memories now based on half-formed foundations, but even the half-truth didn't justify succumbing to their mutual desire for the sake of her peace of mind.

The tiny darts of regret that had stabbed him last night when he'd accepted his own decision returned, sharper this time. Sucking in a breath, he looked down to find her gaze on him, one shapely eyebrow curved. Before they'd met, he hadn't been one for public displays of affection. That had quickly changed with Sienna. The relentless need to touch her, to establish ownership, was an unquenchable fire that burned within him.

Finding that Sienna hadn't shared his new-found need to embrace his ownership had...unsettled him. Truth be told, it had been one of the many out-of-the-norm things that had disconcerted him about their relationship. That still did.

But he intended to handle it.

He saw the question in her eyes now triggered by his withdrawal. Before he could formulate an acceptable response, the lift doors parted on the ground-floor lobby. He wheeled the chair to the edge of the lawn then scooped her up in his arms.

Her breath caught lightly before her hands curled around his neck.

'Are you okay?' she breathed against his ear.

'I should be asking you that.'

'I told you, I'm fine. Whereas you seem...agitated.'

There was a little lingering teasing in her tone, but her face had turned serious.

'Look at the situation we find ourselves in. I think a little bit of agitation is warranted, don't you?'

'*Situation*... You mean the baby?'

He froze to a halt three feet from the chopper. 'The baby is one factor, of course, but I meant you, too.'

She made a half-comical face. 'Am I the first lover of yours to literally lose her mind?'

'Your attempt at hilarity is noted. And rejected.' He stepped into the aircraft and placed her on the back seat. Joining her there, he buckled her seat belt before nodding at his pilot.

When he went to secure his belt, her hand covered his. 'I wasn't trying to make light of the situation. I just...I may not have all my faculties intact, but I can tell you still brood over things. I don't want to be one of the things you brood over. I'm not fragile.'

He couldn't stop the bitterness that twisted inside him. 'Trust me, I already know this.'

'Emiliano—'

'No more talking, Sienna. There will be plenty of time for that. For now, just enjoy the ride.'

At that time of the day there wasn't much to see, save moving headlights on the motorway and then a spiderweb of lights as they flew over London. But she complied, curling her body against his as they headed to the penthouse.

As they swung east, her gaze tracked the iconic landmarks of the Shard and the Gherkin.

'It'll be good to be home,' she murmured.

Even though a bracing gust of guilt blew through him, he concluded that he was doing the right thing. '*Sí*, it will,' he agreed.

Except it wasn't. Alfie, alerted to the situation, showed his concern without giving the game away.

Not so much the large bouquet of flowers that was delivered half an hour after they walked in.

Emiliano's hackles rose the moment he spotted the over-the-top floral display the concierge manager was handing to Alfie. Unfortunately, Sienna spotted them at the same time, too.

'Oh, how pretty,' she gushed to a wary-looking Alfie. 'Are they for me?'

The butler nodded slowly and opened his mouth. Emiliano's single shake of his head had him clamming up, depositing the vase on a nearby table and walking away.

She approached the flowers and began to dig around for a card. Emiliano, close on her heel, found it first. A brief glance confirmed what he suspected about the sender. A wave of anger rising in his chest, he crushed the card and shoved it in his pocket.

'Are you going to let me read the message or tell me who they're from?'

His jaw clenched. 'No.'

'Oh, come on. Somebody's gone to a bit of trouble. The least you can do is—'

'Nothing! He's a nobody. Forget him.'

His harsh condemnation echoed around the room.

Her eyes widened. Then she frowned.

'You're overreacting. You don't normally overreact. Don't ask me how I know. Unless it's a new habit? Or this is more than just flowers? It's the person, isn't it?'

Emiliano realised her probing was unravelling him, reminding him of everything about their relationship—*Dios mio*, when had that word even become normal for him to utter?—that needled him beneath the surface. He sliced his fingers through his hair, the vow he'd made not to hide the truth from her as far as he could suddenly seeming like the worst idea he'd ever had. Still, he toyed with not answering.

Not until she walked up to him and laid a hand on his cheek. 'Tell me,' she insisted with a quiet firmness.

His skin jumped beneath her touch, a hunger flaring in him he had no right to feel. And yet…

'If you insist on knowing, yes. The sender is a headhunter. According to you, he's made it his mission to poach you from me many times.'

'He's *tried*? That means I haven't entertained him. He's probably just trying to get under your skin.'

He turned away, his lip curling. '*Dios mio*, he's succeeding.'

She gave a startled laugh.

'What?' He frowned, failing completely to see the funny side.

'I never thought I'd see the day you'd admit to being anything but totally invincible.'

He shrugged. 'We all have our faults, *querida*. Some of us are better at hiding them than others.'

A puzzled line appeared on her smooth forehead. 'I'm not sure that's a good thing to boast about.'

'Boast or not, it's the simple truth. If your vulnerability or circumstance is constantly exploited, you learn to hide them. And, with everything that comes from frequent practice, you wake up one day to find you excel at it.'

'And in your case it's basic survival?'

'*Was*. I'm invincible now. Remember?'

She laughed, then sobered after a minute. 'Did I know this about you before? You're not telling me something I've forgotten, are you? Because that would upset me.'

Emiliano was hit by a bolt of shock at her naked admission. 'Why would it upset you?'

'Because, if I don't know this about you after a year, then what have we been doing all this time?'

He had a ready answer for that, but to do that he would need to reach into a box he preferred to keep shut for the sake of sanity. 'Rest easy, *pequeña*. This is a revelation of sorts for us both.'

'Wow. And all from a simple bouquet of delphiniums and baby's breath,' she murmured, reaching out to touch the nearest petal.

He scooped the vase out of her reach, curbing the urge to throw it across the room. 'You hate delphiniums. Baby's breath, too.'

She dropped her hand. 'Now you're exaggerating.'

'No, I am not. You're very particular about the flowers you love. These aren't on your list.'

Her eyes widened. 'I have a list?'

Despite his black mood, his mouth twitched. 'You have a list for everything. These flowers didn't make the cut. Which is why they're going in the bin.'

He derived a certain childish satisfaction in trashing the flowers before tracking down his butler. A three-minute revelatory conversation worsened his mood.

David Hunter had been in touch with his concierge several times in the last day, seemingly after an extensive search for Sienna. He had to give the man credit for his investigative skills. But that was where Emiliano's tolerance started and ended. Hunter had balls, sending flowers to a woman at her lover's apartment.

Ex-lover.

Whatever.

Emiliano had been hustled into letting her go before he was ready, not that he doubted he would have done so eventually.

Whereas Hunter was overstepping. Unless he felt an entitlement towards Sienna that extended beyond just hopeful interest…

Emiliano's teeth clenched tight as the possible answers to that question reeled through his mind.

Questions he couldn't ask.

Exhaling to restore much-needed control, he issued a new set of instructions to his butler, one that included prohibiting David Hunter from coming anywhere near his building, and returned to the living room.

'I've decided,' he announced, his thoughts sifting through pros and cons and demolishing every obstacle in his way.

Sienna turned in a graceful movement, her slender body drawing and keeping his attention.

'What?'

'A change of scene will do you good. Tomorrow, we're going to take the jet, head to Paris for New Year, then we're going island hopping around the Caribbean until you get disgustingly homesick and beg me to bring you back.'

Her full lips parted in surprise, then a light frown marred her forehead. 'But… What about work? You can't just take off.'

'I'm the boss,' he said. 'I can do whatever I want, work from any continent I choose.'

'What about me? I can't just—'

'Yes, you can. I decree it, so you're signed off indefinitely. Besides, it's the holidays. And you love the islands at this time of year. It made the top of your list, I believe.'

Her smile was wide and blinding, tugging at him in places he didn't want tugged. But still, he stood in place as she swayed towards him and rose on her bare feet to slide her arms around his neck.

'Okay, then, if the boss decrees it…'

'He does.'

'Then I'm all yours.'

He tried to keep his face and voice neutral, despite the thick pounding in his veins. '*Sí*…you are.' The possessive punch in his tone was to do with the child nestling in her womb he told himself. Nothing more.

'But I bet you get homesick before I do.'

'Care to put your money where your mouth is?'

Her gaze dropped to his mouth and he fought to suppress a groan. The eyes that met his were a darker shade of green. And the voice that responded was a sultry one that dared. 'Bring it.'

CHAPTER SEVEN

'Emiliano?'

'Hmm?' His voice was a deep, sexy rumble that drew a delicious shiver through her.

Before her, Paris was spread out in stunning electric light, the hour before the year ended and a brand new one began filling the cold night air with palpable excitement. From their bird's-eye view from the top of their magnificent five-star hotel, it truly felt as if the world itself was laid out at their feet.

She had no recollection of previous visits to Paris, although Emiliano had informed her there had been a few. It disturbed her not to remember, but the idea of falling in love all over again with the romantic city wasn't too bad, so she embraced it.

The discreet terrace heater nearby was designed to keep the worst of the chill out of the air, but Emiliano had draped a cashmere blanket over her shoulders a moment ago, then stayed close when she'd tucked his arms around her. On the low wall in front of them, her glass of sparkling water stood next to his flute of champagne and behind them, in the living room of their presidential suite, soft sounds of French Christmas carols lent even more magic to the night.

Her sense of contentment should've been complete, but she couldn't dismiss the disquiet blooming within her.

'What is it, Sienna?' he pressed after a minute had gone by.

She hesitated, unwilling to taint the night with unwelcome conversation, but she couldn't hold it in, so she blurted out the question that had been looming large in her potholed mind for the last twenty-four hours. 'Why weren't the hospital staff able to locate any of my family?'

She felt him tense and for a second she regretted voicing her question now instead of later.

His breath stirred the top of her head and he pulled the cashmere blanket tighter around her. 'Don't worry about that right now.'

She shook her head, turning in his arms to look up into his face. 'Tell me, please. Otherwise I'll imagine the worst…' Her words drifted off when she caught sight of the regret in his eyes. 'It *is* bad, isn't it?'

'Sienna…'

'Are we estranged? Was it my fault? I can't imagine falling out with every member of my family, though. Unless my family is small. Even so, it's New Year's. Why would they not want to see me at—'

'Stop.' His voice was firm. 'No, there is no estrangement. There is no abandonment because…' He stopped, his jaw flexing for a moment. 'Because there is no family. Not one I could find, anyway.'

Pain and shock robbed her of breath for a moment. 'What? Why? Did…something happen?' She almost dreaded asking as much as she dreaded the answer.

His arms tightened convulsively around her. 'This is not the type of conversation I envisioned to usher in the New Year.'

She braced her hands on his chest, shamelessly taking strength from the steady beats of his heart. 'Then let's finish it quickly.' She saw the obstinate look in his eyes and pressed harder. 'Please, Emiliano.'

'I had my investigators look into your past these last couple of weeks.'

She frowned, her disquiet growing. 'You mean, I never told you?'

His face tightened, a neutral expression sliding over his features.

'You might as well tell me everything, Emiliano. My life is one giant question mark right now. I can't help that, but I don't want to bring this one into the New Year, either.'

He remained silent for so long she thought she'd lost the argument. His chest rose and fell beneath her hands. 'We never shared our pasts with each other. We preferred it that way. So, no, I don't know enough about your history to tell you why I couldn't find any family for you.'

The words, although stated evenly, still landed with cold brutality, probably because, contrary to what she'd imagined, she was nowhere near ready for them. 'I... Oh, God... What if I don't have any?' She didn't realise she'd swayed and slumped against him until he swore under his breath and gathered her even closer.

'This was a bad idea,' he stated grimly. That peculiar note was back in his voice again, but when she stared up at him his expression remained unreadable.

She shook her head. For several minutes she couldn't speak, the sheer starkness of her existence almost too much to bear. 'I, well, I'm glad you told me...'

A rough sound rumbled from his throat. 'Are you?'

She nodded despite the abject news. 'I don't want secrets between us.'

His jaw clenched for a taut second before his arms tightened around her. 'And I don't wish anything to stand in the way of your recovery, so I reserve the right to veto any questions or demands. *Sí?*' The demand was domineering.

She wanted to say yes, but a knot inside her refused to unravel. 'I can't help but think, if you hadn't been there for me when I was in hospital, I would've been alone...'

His grip tightened a fraction. 'But you are *not* alone. You are here. With me.'

She heard the words, wanted to bask in their possessive warmth, but she couldn't shake the confusion as to why she would keep secrets from this man who made her heart beat with wild desire every time he looked at her. She couldn't imagine he would let her keep something so important from him.

Unless he wasn't interested?

The question came from nowhere, slammed with force into her and left her floundering. She watched his nostrils flare, felt a new restlessness tinge the atmosphere. 'Why didn't I tell you about my past?'

He shrugged. 'Family isn't a subject either of us likes to dwell on. I left you to your reasons. Mine were…inconsequential.'

'Inconsequential?'

'*Sí*, and enough about this matter, too. I've answered your questions. Just bear in mind that, whether you do have family or not, it isn't uncommon to feel completely alone even in the largest of so-called families. It might look rosy and whole from the outside looking in, but appearances are often deceptive.' His tone held a trace of bitterness that brought her up short and bruised her heart.

She'd been firing questions at him with no regard for his own circumstances.

'Emiliano…'

She stopped when a muted roar rose from street level. Turning her head, she saw the countdown clock superimposed on the Eiffel Tower.

Thirty seconds until the old year was put to bed and a new one ushered in.

Firm hands touched her cheek, redirecting her focus to the powerful man in front of her. 'You're carrying my child. A child whose needs should come first. This is what should be at the forefront of our minds. Are you prepared to do that?'

'Of course. I want this baby. More than anything.'

'Then no more dwelling on the past, *si*? From this moment forward, we look to the future. Agreed?'

'*Dix, neuf, huit, sept, six...*'

Sienna held her breath as the clock counted out the last seconds. Exhaling in a muted rush, she nodded. 'Agreed.'

Fireworks burst into the night sky, drenching the heavens with colour as a loud cheer cannoned across the city. Eyes of dark gold held her captive, bore into hers, before drifting over her face to rest on her mouth.

'Happy New Year, *querida*,' he murmured huskily.

Her heart lurched wildly then banged hard against her ribs. 'Happy New Year, Emiliano,' she replied, her voice equally hoarse, draped with unvoiced hopes and desires. Catching one of the hands binding her, she linked it with hers and pressed them gently against her belly. 'Happy New Year, Baby Castillo.'

Emiliano inhaled sharply. After a moment, his hand freed hers to splay over her belly in a display so potently possessive, she would've protested had she not completely revelled in it. In the tumult of the past couple of days, many questions had plagued her. One she hadn't been brave enough to confront was how Emiliano felt about this unplanned pregnancy. With his words, his touch, a part of her settled. They needed to have a more in-depth conversation at some point down the line, but she was prepared to rest her mind on that score for now.

Caught in the maelstrom of emotions she couldn't name, she raised her gaze to his. One desire in particular rose to the fore, the need pounding through her as forcefully as the pyrotechnic display thundering overhead. Locking her fingers at his nape, she pressed herself against him. 'Kiss me,' she begged.

A strangled sound emitted from his throat a second before he shook his head. 'No, Sienna.' His voice held pained reluctance.

Had she not felt the evidence of his formidable need against her belly, or the blazing hunger in his eyes, she would've thought he didn't want her. She could only conclude that his reluctance stemmed from somewhere else.

'It's okay. I'm not fragile. I passed all the tests the doctor put me through this evening.' Despite her protests, Emiliano had refused to leave London without a doctor and nurse accompanying them on his private jet to monitor her every twinge. After much negotiation, they'd agreed on a check-up every twelve hours.

A grimace tautened his face. 'Nevertheless, I don't think you should—'

'A kiss isn't going to harm me, Emiliano. Not when it'll make me…happy.'

A deep shudder shook his frame. *'Dios mío. Esto es el infierno.'*

This is hell.

She didn't stop to ponder how she understood his words. Or why a simple kiss was so hard for him. It probably had something to do with the fact that nothing between them felt simple. All she knew was that he was still denying her a kiss. And she was being consumed by the desire for it.

'Please. Isn't it tradition to kiss the one you're with at the stroke of the New Year? I won't break, I promise.'

A short bark of self-deprecating laughter rolled out before he inhaled deeply. 'You don't know what you're asking.'

'Yes, I do. And I'm not taking no for an answer.'

She'd barely finished speaking when he gave a pained groan, spiked his hands into her hair and slanted his mouth over hers. Hot, potent and more exhilarating than the fireworks still echoing around them, Emiliano's kiss was intensely thrilling and completely addictive. With a deep, thankful moan, she opened her mouth beneath his, granting him the possessive entry he sought without hesitation.

He kissed her with an expertise that resonated all the way to her toes and back up again. When his tongue danced with hers, the flames—already stoked high with anticipation—rose higher, threatening to consume her.

Breasts aching, sensitive nipples peaked with shameless arousal, it was all she could do to whimper and hold on as sensation soared. Sienna wondered if it was the hormones raging through her that made this kiss more special than any she'd shared with Emiliano before, but by the time the need for oxygen drove them apart she was trembling from head to toe. Trembling and on the point of tears.

'Sienna?' A thick vein of alarm threaded his voice as he stared down at her.

Chagrined, she brushed away a tear. 'It's…I'm okay. Hell, I don't even know why I'm crying.'

'Maldición,' he swore thickly before he swung her up in his arms.

Striding through the opulent suite fit for a king, he entered the master bedroom.

Tugging the blanket from around her shoulders, he crouched before her and slid off her stone-coloured platform shoes. Her cream wrap-around dress, secured by a simple tie, came loose with a single pull. Sliding it off her, he tossed it onto a nearby chaise before striding into the dressing room and returning with a silk nightie.

In the bathroom, he stood next to the vanity, watching with eagle eyes as she brushed her teeth.

By the time they re-entered the bedroom, irritation was beginning to take hold.

'I can put myself to bed, Emiliano. And you can stop beating yourself up about the kiss, too. This…' she indicated her drying tears '…is just pregnancy hormones.'

He paused a second before he carried on his self-imposed task of disrobing her. 'It wouldn't have been triggered if I'd kept my hands off you,' he stated grimly.

'You've had your hands on me in one form or another since we left the hospital. You take my hand and walk me to a chair when I enter a room. You tuck my hair behind my ear when I'm talking to you and you can't see my face properly. And who dressed me tonight, despite me saying I was quite capable of putting my own dress on?'

A wave of shock washed over his features before his brows clamped in a dark frown and his features shuttered. 'You have my apologies. I'll be more careful in the future.'

She let out an exasperated breath. 'I don't want you to be careful!' Pulling back the sheets with a little more force than necessary, she slid into bed. 'I'm fine with all of it, Emiliano. I just don't want you treating me like I'm made of delicate glass because we kissed.'

'Calm down.'

'I am calm,' she said, then took another steadying breath, the corner of the luxurious bedspread twisting between her fingers. 'The way you treat me…I feel as if I'm missing something vital, which is ironic, considering I only have a fraction of my mind working correctly.'

'Your mind is fine,' he stated in a tone that said he wouldn't welcome challenge on that declaration.

She sighed, a thread of weariness weaving into her limbs despite her protest. 'We'll agree to disagree. For now. But I reserve the right to resume—and *win*—this point.'

One corner of his mouth twitched even though the forbidding expression remained. 'I don't doubt it. Your superb cognitive skills were the reason you were my vice-president of Acquisitions.'

She frowned. *'Were?'*

He froze for an infinitesimal second. *'Sí,* before your accident.'

'Oh. Right. I suppose I can't return to work now with my mind the way it is.'

His jaw clenched. 'You can't return to work because

you've been through a trauma. From which you're recovering while carrying a baby. You won't be gracing the inside of a boardroom with your presence anytime soon.'

'Is this my boss or my lover talking?' Her challenge was half-hearted, the warm sheets seducing her into sliding deeper, pulling the duvet to her chin.

'It's the man who has a vested interest in your wellbeing. The man who also intends to win his argument, and a few more besides, when the time comes.'

She didn't want to start another argument, or delve beneath the somewhat cryptic remarks, simply because her eyelids were growing heavier by the minute. And also because she'd become painfully aware that Emiliano was making no move to undress and join her in bed. He'd taken to sleeping in the adjoining bedroom, while Alfie and the medical staff slept in the suite next door.

It was a situation she'd hoped would be altered come New Year. But it seemed her hopes were to be dashed when he stared down at her for a long moment before he stepped back with a resolute expression.

'Sleep well, Sienna.'

He was gone before she could respond in kind. As, she discovered an hour later, was the sleep she'd thought would be quick in coming.

Changing positions for the umpteenth time, she replayed the evening in her mind, including the kiss, memory of which still glowed like embers inside her. Sienna wished the heat of that kiss could erase the cold reality of the past Emiliano had divulged.

There was no record of a family out there.

For all intents and purposes, and until her memory supplied her with the information, she only had Emiliano, the man she would be connected to for ever through their baby.

The man who consciously didn't want to touch her. Telling herself her condition was very much a factor and that it was early days didn't soothe the tiny prickles of anxiety within her.

Something was wrong. And, if she couldn't rely on her memory to supply her with the *whys*, she'd just have to find another way.

Emiliano threw back the cognac he'd poured for himself before settling in his study chair to place the call. He didn't dread it—he was too much of a pragmatist for that—but he wasn't relishing it, either. All he knew was that it needed to be done. The twinge of guilt that lanced him for letting Matias down was ruthlessly suppressed. He would find another way to help Graciela and make it up to his brother if…*when*… Matias emerged from his coma.

He entered the number from memory, surprised he still retained it. It was answered on the third ring.

'It's about time you called,' his father said by way of greeting.

Emiliano barely managed to stop his lip from curling. 'You forget that I am the one coming to your rescue. A little appreciation wouldn't go amiss.'

His father hesitated a moment before he spoke, and Emiliano was gratified to hear the less belligerent tone. 'We haven't heard a word from you, save a call from your assistant to say you'd be in touch. That was a week ago. We were…concerned.'

'My life doesn't stop simply because yours is in free fall.' He didn't see the need to mention his own life had been in free fall, too, from the moment he'd returned from Argentina.

He heard his father clear his throat and refocused. 'Rodrigo Cabrera has been expecting your call. He feels insulted to be kept waiting. He's being hounded by the press for an official announcement.'

'He should've thought of that before he planted his tabloid hacks to create a relationship that doesn't exist.'

'A relationship you agreed to.' He heard the definite note of panic in his father's voice.

'My only agreement was to have dinner with his daughter in the hope of convincing her to talk some sense into her father and get him to drop this whole ridiculous situation before it went any further. What I should've done was walk away then.' If he had, he wouldn't be in this situation.

'But you didn't.' The panic was much more pronounced. 'You made promises, which Cabrera wants you to honour now.'

Emiliano's hand tightened on the handset, the knowledge that he wasn't as immune to his father's distress as he'd like to be making his jaw clench. 'That is not going to happen. We need to find another way to deal with the matter of your debt.'

'Impossible. I have an agreement with Cabrera.'

'An agreement that had neither my knowledge nor consent. An agreement you forced on Matias. Did you stop to think how your selfishness would impact on him, or did you blithely sign away his life the way you're attempting to sign away mine?'

'What are you talking about?'

'Do you even know where Matias was going when he crashed?'

'Of course I know. He was on his way to conduct Castillo business—'

'No, he was on his way to the airport after ending things with his girlfriend. He destroyed his relationship with her in order to save your skin.'

The irony of the full circle his family seemed to have come would've been laughable if it wasn't so eerily spine-chilling. Except, this time, he wasn't the one who'd fallen into a coma. It was the mother of his child. The woman whose presence in his life hinged on the absence of her memories. The knot that had resided in his gut for far longer than he cared to contemplate threatened to unravel. Ruthlessly, he grappled it into place.

'Your brother understood the true meaning of family and sacrifice, whereas you don't seem to have second thoughts about breaking your—'

'Save it, old man. You lost your right to guilt me into submission a very long time ago. And don't speak of Matias in the past tense. You may have written him off, but I haven't.'

'Have some respect, boy,' his father bristled. 'You wouldn't exist without me.'

He wouldn't exist. The words struck a deep chord within him, causing his fingers to fist on his desk.

Yes, his father was responsible for bringing him into the world. Just as he himself was now responsible for another. Only, Emiliano didn't intend to be little more than a biological footnote in his child's life.

He would be more.

He didn't know how, but would be *better*. He wouldn't fail or ignore his child as he had been failed and ignored.

'Are you listening to me?'

His attention refocused, sharpened until his intent was as clear as the finest crystal. 'I'm listening and I'm hearing you, but I don't think *you* are hearing me. The deal with Cabrera as it stands doesn't work for me. He can accept my financial terms, or I'm prepared to hear him out if he has an alternative that suits me. But marrying his daughter is irrevocably off the table.'

'Why?' his father demanded.

'Because I'm getting married to someone else.'

CHAPTER EIGHT

'*Buenos días, cariño.*'

'*Buenos días, guapo. Has dormido bien?*'

Emiliano froze in surprise and stared at the woman bathed in sunlight on the terrace of his villa.

'You speak Spanish?' he asked.

A light flush tinged her cheeks before she responded hesitantly, '*Un poco, pero estoy tratando.*'

He carried on walking towards her, his senses reeling a little as he pulled out the chair and joined her at the breakfast table. In the typical style of the woman who'd managed his acquisitions with exemplary intelligence, she'd perfected the nuance and intonation of his mother tongue, and even found a way to thread sensuality through the words. 'You're more than trying,' he responded, noting the gruffness in his voice. 'You excel at it.'

She grinned before a plump segment of mango found its way into her mouth. Watching her tongue dart out to lick a drop of juice from the corner of her mouth lit an instant fire in his groin. Combined with the white bikini set clinging to her body, its existence poorly disguised by the see-through mesh sarong, he knew the next half hour would be a true test of his control.

They'd been on his private island off the coast of the Bahamas a little over a week. Each day had brought the challenge of seeing her in a different swimsuit and wrestling with the increasingly uncontrollable urge to touch her. It also hadn't gone past his notice that her costumes were getting skimpier with each passing day.

It was the reason he'd banished the villa's employees to the staff bungalow yesterday. Only Alfie was allowed into the main residence without express permission, the fact that he was gay barely giving him a pass.

'How long have you been keeping this from me?' he asked, concentrating all his efforts on pouring steaming black coffee…slowly…to take his mind off the satin-soft skin on display.

Her smile widened, still blindingly beautiful, her green eyes lighting up. 'I woke up this morning and the memory just appeared. I remembered I'd been listening to tapes, although I can't remember where I got them from or how long I've been learning. I'm guessing from your reaction that you didn't know, so… Surprise!'

The rigid tension charging through his body made him wonder how he was managing to set the coffee pot down without breaking it. 'No, I didn't know. And, yes, it's a wonderful surprise.' He paused a beat, then asked off-handedly, 'Did you remember anything else?'

Her smile dimmed then switched off completely. A vice tightened viciously around his chest. He wanted to pre-empt the words that she was about to utter with…something. But none were forthcoming. So he sat and awaited the falling axe.

'I…I know now why no one came to see me at the hospital. Besides you.'

His gaze probed her face, noted her distress. 'Tell me,' he encouraged, the need to know overcoming whatever consequences lay in his future.

Her gaze dropped. He fought the urge to nudge her delicate chin up and watched her.

'I remember my childhood. I'm an orphan, Emiliano. I was left with nuns at a children's mission in Surrey when I was a baby. My first name was folded into my baby blanket. The nuns gave me a last name.'

She gave a laugh that sounded surprisingly similar to the one that coughed up whenever he thought of his own childhood. 'I was abandoned by a mother who only stopped long enough to scribble a name she thought was appropriate for the child she didn't want to raise before disappearing.'

Her hand dropped to her stomach and her face twisted in anguish for a brief second. 'So that's my history. And now you know.'

Despite her words, the eyes that met his held a touch of vulnerability that had him going against his better judgement and capturing her chin in his hand.

'And it changes nothing. You are who you are, regardless of the mystery of your birth. Even armed with full knowledge of one's birth, there are never any guarantees of affection or acceptance.'

She blinked, her full mouth trembling for a few moments before her head rose and the strength and determination he'd glimpsed many times across his boardroom table powered her spine straight.

Nodding, she said, 'I remembered something else.'

Emiliano swallowed hard. And again. *'Qué?'* The question was a rough croak.

'Switzerland.'

'What about Switzerland?'

Troubled eyes rested on him. 'I remembered that your brother is in a coma. We went to visit him on the way back from Prague. In July…?'

It was a disgrace to feel the enormous relief that punched through him. But he'd never professed to be perfect. Relief tingling through his extremities, he picked up his cup and took a gulp of coffee. *'Sí,* that's correct.'

'Is he… Has there been any change?'

Recalling the last time she'd asked him the same question, Emiliano schooled his features before he shook his head. 'I visited him two weeks ago. There's been no change. The doctors are debating whether to try an experimental procedure to wake him.'

Her breath caught. 'Is it risky?'

'Every procedure carries an element of risk, but they think he can withstand it. His brain activity is promising. The doctors believe he should be awake by now.'

'So are they going to do it?'

He took another sip of coffee before he answered. All he tasted was bitterness. 'If I had my way, they would do it tomorrow. Matias needs to wake up and live his life. Unfortunately, my parents have to provide consent. They're… debating the matter.' The raw anger eating through him that Matias's life was wasting away because of his parents' indecision mounted.

'What? Why? I would've thought any parent would jump at the chance to see their child well.' Her genuine puzzlement and response settled something inside him he hadn't even been aware needed tending.

Or perhaps he had. His own silent floundering about his ability to be a father had also thrown up questions about the mother of his child. He didn't doubt Sienna would rise to the challenge of motherhood with the same vigour she'd brought to his company…should she choose to, once her memory returned.

And there was the other conundrum. Sienna might be excited about the pregnancy now, but what would happen in the future, when perhaps she would conclude that he fell short of the task of being a father?

Emiliano knew first-hand that love for one child didn't necessarily transmit to another. For the longest time, he'd tried to unravel that particular puzzle in his own circumstances, until he'd realised he was wasting his time.

Warm fingers touched the back of his hand, bringing him back to the present and her questions.

'Because keeping Matias the way he is now keeps him alive and safe, which is an appropriate action any parent would consider on behalf of their child. But their indecision also serves the dual purpose of elevating me to the position of temporary firstborn, which means his responsibilities become mine.'

Her eyes had been growing rounder with consternation with each utterance. 'Are you saying they're using him as a *pawn*?'

A few weeks ago, he would've given an unequivocal affirmation. 'Perhaps not deliberately, but I can't hide from the evidence that their indecision plays to their advantage while keeping him in a glass box,' he ground out through the tide of fury blanketing him. He'd yet to find a way to circumvent the current impasse with his parents. But he would. His brother deserved better than the hand his parents were dealing him.

'Has it always been like this between you and them? The distance and the…bitterness?'

'Until Matias's accident, I hadn't seen or spoken to them for over ten years. I left home the day I turned eighteen.'

'Why?' she asked softly, passing him a peeled orange before reaching for a warm croissant.

He took his time to chew and swallow, certain the dull ache in his chest was residual anger from the situation with Matias. His history with his parents was dead and buried. 'I realised very early on in life that Matias was the chosen son. That I was merely the spare, brought and paraded as and when I was needed, but otherwise there was very little use for me.'

There was no trace of a smile on her face now, only naked anguish. For him. 'Oh, Emiliano. I'm sorry,' she murmured.

Her voice soothed him. *She* soothed him. So he found himself continuing. 'I don't think they even noticed the day I left.'

Her green eyes turned stormy dark. 'That's not true. I'm sure they did.'

A long-forgotten conversation with his brother unspooled in his mind. 'Perhaps. Matias told me once they asked about me. But they didn't care enough to pick up the phone. Not once.' He shrugged, but the gesture didn't quite flow.

'Did Matias ever try to talk you out of leaving?'

He nodded, the recollection opening a new vein of pain he'd thought healed. 'Many times in the weeks before, when I told him of my plans. I think it hurt him more to admit he was our parents' favourite. When he realised my bags were packed, and that I would leave with or without his help, he gave up.'

Her face pinched in deeper sympathy and for several moments Emiliano wondered why he hadn't told her this before, why he was choosing now to tell a story that he'd buried so deep.

It wasn't as simple as not having other things such as work or sex in the way. No, sex was very much on his mind. *Dios mío*, he only had to catch a glimpse of her chest rising and falling to feel his temperature soaring. And ever since he'd walked onto the terrace his fingers had been itching to sink into her thick, luxurious hair and kiss her the way he'd done at New Year.

But he admitted there was an openness to this version of Sienna that appealed to him. It made talking to her easier. Made him want to reach out to her... Hell, maybe be a better version of himself, too?

He mentally shrugged, took the buttered croissant she'd set in front of him and took a large bite. For a few minutes they fell into easy silence as they mulled over his revelations.

She picked up another pastry and buttered it for herself but didn't eat it. Instead, she glanced back up at him through long lashes. 'So, where did you go? What did you do after you left?'

'I'd planned on staying in Buenos Aires, finding whatever job I could. But Matias had other ideas.'

'Oh?'

'He drove me to the airport and handed me a ticket to London. He'd enrolled me in night school so I could continue my education and got me a paid internship at a financial institution.'

'Oh, my God, that's amazing.'

His throat clogged for a brief moment. '*Sí*, he was...*is*... amazing. The only thing he wanted in return was that I wouldn't forget our family, and that I would offer my help should he need it. He didn't ask for over ten years.'

'So we were both abandoned, in our own way, by those who should've cared for us,' she mused quietly, her croissant now in shredded pieces on her plate.

He hadn't taken the time to make that connection, but now he nodded, a swell of feeling widening inside him as he stared into her eyes. 'But we have risen above it, *sí*?' Her nod wasn't altogether convincing. And, when her green eyes clouded over again, he leaned towards her. 'What is it?'

'I can't help but wonder if our scars will affect our child somehow.'

He was shaking his head before she'd finished speaking, everything inside him rejecting the possibility of that notion. 'We will do better for our child, *querida*. On this you have my full promise.'

He cursed under his breath as her mouth gave the faintest tremble before tears filled her eyes. 'You're crying again.' God, he was becoming a master at stating the obvious. In his defence, he'd never been faced with a tearful Sienna in the year they'd been together. He grimly admitted that this was yet another thing that pushed him right out of his comfort zone.

She waved him away before swiping at her cheeks. 'I'm

fine. I told you, my emotions are a little heightened, that's all. And, yes, this time it's definitely your fault.'

'For throwing my unsavoury skeletons at your feet?'

She rolled her eyes, rose from her chair and slid sinuously into his lap. Emiliano stifled a desperate groan as her arms wound themselves around his neck. She smelled of lemongrass sunscreen and pure, intoxicating woman. And he was drowning in the hunger that shook through him. 'For easing my fear that this baby isn't going to regret having me as a mother one day.'

Another knot unravelled. 'Your concern means you care, so he will be lucky to call you Mama,' he replied gruffly, the hands he'd ordered to stay at his sides somehow finding their way up her thighs and over her hips.

She bent forward until their noses were almost touching. '*She* will be equally blessed to have you as her father,' she whispered, another well of tears filling her eyes.

He gently brushed them away with his thumb. 'Enough with these tears, *querida*. I don't like them.'

'Okay, Emiliano, I'll do my best not to bother you with my unsightly tears,' she said, her breath washing over his lips. The plump curves of her mouth were a lesson in raw temptation. As were the nipples peaking beneath her flimsy bikini top.

'There's nothing unsightly about you, *guapa*.'

'The scars on my skull tell a different story, but I'm prepared to let you win this argument. *Gracias, hermoso.*'

Emiliano decide there and then that, with her soft voice echoing in his head, he would encourage her learning so she would only speak to him in Spanish. He also decided for the second time since he sat down that he was fine with not being perfect. Because *not* kissing her right then, denying himself the pleasure of her soft lips, was one ask too far.

So he lowered his head and tasted the sweetest nectar

known to man. Her response was unfettered and immediate. As if, like him, she'd been caught in the talons of
hunger for far too long. He took her mouth the way other,
more ravenous parts of him wanted to take her body.

She whimpered, moaned and pressed closer until a red
haze of arousal overtook his entire world.

He needed to stop before things went too far. He'd come
out here to discuss their future with her. A discussion that
required delicate handling. Following the words he'd spoken to his father—words he hadn't realised had been on the
tip of his tongue before he'd spoken them, but had known
immediately that he would act upon—he'd been biding his
time until Sienna was stronger. The week on his island had
worked wonders for her, a brief bout of morning sickness
lasting a few short days before abating.

He'd thought long and hard about waiting for her memory to return before going ahead with his plans, but the
doctor had reiterated that they were dealing with a piece of
string of indeterminate length where that was concerned.

And, with each day that passed, Emiliano was losing
the conviction that waiting was the better option. Whatever the future held, they were having this baby. And, before the issue with his fake engagement had broken them
apart, they'd been content together. He wasn't willing to
accept that that was gone for ever.

So he kissed her, infusing his need into the act until she
was breathless and pliant against him. Only then did he
pull away to look into her desire-drugged eyes.

Yes, he was doing the right thing.

'I have to touch base on a few things this morning, but
come out on the boat with me this evening,' he invited,
after taking another all-too-brief kiss.

A smile lit up every dark place inside him. 'Where are
we sailing to this time?'

His hands moved from her hair to her shoulders, down

her warm, silky skin, and it was all he could do not to pick her up and find the nearest bed.

All in good time.

'It's a surprise.'

The package he'd requested had arrived from Turks and Caicos late last night. The rest of the preparation would be underway soon enough. Before then, he needed to step up his investigations on Cabrera, find a weak spot to use to his advantage.

He rose with Sienna still in his arms. It disturbed him that she still weighed much less than he was used to, but the staff were under strict instructions to reverse that situation. And so far she wasn't objecting to being fattened up.

'Where are you taking me?'

He didn't miss the slightly breathless anticipation in her voice. He nearly altered his course, only the stern voice warning him to do this right keeping his compass true.

'To your second-favourite spot on the island.'

Although she made a tiny face when he rounded the terrace and made a beeline for the pool, she laughed. 'And my first is?'

'A certain king-sized bed, of course. Your happy snores shake the whole house at night.'

She thumped his shoulder playfully as he set her down at the lounger next to the table which had been set up with a cooler of drinks and several snacks. He knew Alfie would be out like clockwork every hour to make sure she didn't want for anything.

Taking a step from him, she untied the knot and dropped her sarong.

'Madre de Dios, tener compasión.'

Her very shameless, very feminine grin as she caught her hair up to secure it in a loose bun atop her head told him she relished her effect on him and wasn't interested in the mercy he pleaded for. Her gaze dropped to the very visible, very inconvenient evidence of his arousal before rising to his. He was gratified to see her quickening breath.

'Hasta la vista, cariño.'

She bit her lip as she turned away and spread her delicious body out on the lounger. He needed to leave, head back inside, but he stayed for one more look. And, as his gaze paused on the barest hint of roundness at her abdomen, that well of feeling in his chest expanded.

Yes, he was doing the right thing. All he had to do now was to secure her agreement.

At the stroke of six, Sienna heard a light knock on her bedroom door. She turned away from the mirror, loving the way the loose white sleeveless dress floated around her body before the hem dropped to her ankles. On her feet, she wore gold flip-flops, her deeper desire to go barefoot overridden by common sense. The path around the villa to the jetty where the launch would take them to Emiliano's yacht was a little gravelly. She couldn't risk twisting an ankle or falling on her behind.

Flipping her hair over her shoulders, she quickly secured the gold hoop earrings and answered the door.

Alfie stood on the threshold dressed in a smart white tunic and dark trousers.

'I've come to escort you to your date,' he said, offering his arm.

Although his smile was easy now, she'd caught a questioning look in his eyes in the past week which she'd shrugged off. She knew he and the rest of the staff had been given an abbreviated version of her illness and instructed to take special care of her. They weren't intrusive and every assistance offered to ensure she took care of her baby's health was welcome, so she didn't mind.

He conversed easily with her as they went down the long hallway to the grand staircase leading to the stunning hallway. Solid light oak floors polished to the highest gleam beautifully complemented whitewashed walls decorated with nautical blues and greens that gave the extensive luxury villa a fresh vibrancy. Every glass door and shuttered window was built to slide aside during the day to let in the salt-tinged breeze from the sea. According to Emiliano, the first time she'd set foot on Castillo Island, she'd remarked that the inside of the villa made her feel as though she were walking on sunshine and she couldn't help but smile now as she walked outside and inhaled the fresh, clean air.

Along the path that led past the garden to the beach, small flame lamps had been positioned to guide their way. Crickets chirped among the colourful plants, and palm trees swayed softly overhead. Although her gaze touched on and absorbed the heady paradise surrounding her, her senses leaped eagerly, fast-forwarding to the evening ahead.

To Emiliano.

She'd spent most of the day outside but her thoughts had dwelt very much on the innermost secrets he'd revealed to her and the secret hope in her heart that she wasn't afraid to admit to herself any longer.

She wanted Emiliano. Wanted to be with him, to claim him in the most primal way possible. It had nothing to do with the baby and everything to do with the fact that she recognised and accepted her deeper feelings for him.

She didn't know whether she was ready to put a label on how she felt or even probe it past mere acceptance. For now, she was going to acknowledge its existence. Maybe nurture it with care and attention.

Emiliano stood waiting at the end of the twenty-foot-long jetty. He wore casual white trousers teamed with stylish loafers. The sleeves of his open-necked white linen shirt were folded back to reveal strong muscular arms bronzed by the sun. At some point the breeze had ruffled his hair, lending him a raffish air that threatened to blow her composure to smithereens.

Intense eyes tracked her progress from path to launch, his hand extending to her as she reached him.

He took both of her hands in his and kissed each cheek. Her heart tripped over itself as he shamelessly inhaled her scent before tucking her hair back to rasp in her ear, '*Buenas noches*, Sienna. You look breathtaking.'

Suddenly tongue-tied, she smiled and murmured, 'Thank you,' as Alfie readied the launch.

They didn't have far to go, only a mile or so to where Emiliano's superyacht was anchored in deeper waters. The vessel was a stunning masterpiece, its sleek white-and-silver lines spotlighted by coloured lights that magnified its beauty in the early-evening sun. She'd been on board twice since they arrived and each time she hadn't failed to be awed by the craftsmanship.

She hadn't made a 'wow' list yet, but she was sure the yacht would make the top ten. Of course, the item that would top that particular list would be the man whose hand rested on her waist to guide her up a short flight of stairs to the middle deck. There at the open-air end a candlelit table had been set, complete with crystal goblets and sterling silverware.

A member of staff hovered nearby. At Emiliano's nod, he stepped forward with a tray holding two coconut drinks. Accepting the drink, she sipped, giving a pleased little moan as exotic flavours exploded on her tongue.

She was about to take another sip when she felt a slight jolt. They were moving. About to ask where they were headed, she remembered it was a surprise. So she followed Emiliano when he took her hand and walked her to the railing, enjoying her drink as they sailed towards the setting sun.

'It's so beautiful here,' she murmured in hushed awe.

'Yes, it is.'

She turned and looked at him. His gaze was on the horizon, but it met hers a second later, his lips curving in a smile that tugged wildly at her heart.

'I take it then that you're not homesick yet?'

The urge to blurt out that she would never be homesick as long as she was with him was caught back at the last moment. Her feelings were still new and untried. She didn't want to risk exposing them to scrutiny yet.

'No, not yet. But I have been wondering about having a scan, though.'

His gaze sharpened. 'Is something wrong?'

She shook her head quickly. 'No, but according to the pregnancy books I'm due for one about now.' Since learning that, she'd been quietly excited about hearing her child's heartbeat for the first time.

Emiliano's fierce expression eased a touch. 'If that's what you want, we don't have to leave. I can have that organised for you here.'

She grinned. 'Careful, or you'll have me thinking you want to keep me barefoot and pregnant here for ever.'

Tawny eyes raked her from head to foot before he shrugged. 'The idea isn't unappealing.'

She laughed. Although he joined her, she caught a serious look in his eyes that twanged a brain cell. Unbidden, she was thrown back to their night in Paris, when she'd sensed an undercurrent in his mood. After searching his expression and seeing nothing but heated interest, she shrugged off the feeling.

As they finished their drinks, they settled into easy conversation, which continued when they sat down to dinner. Chilli-and-lemon-flavoured grilled calamari sharpened her appetite for the chicken and rice dish that followed.

She looked up in surprise when Emiliano stood after their plates were cleared away.

'Don't look so disappointed, *belleza*. We're having dessert over there.'

She followed his pointing finger to a deserted beach where a wide picnic blanket was illuminated by two tall, flaming lamps. Below them, Alfie was readying the launch. She held on to Emiliano's hand as he guided her back downstairs and into it. A few minutes later, he was swinging her into his arms and treading shallow water towards the beach. Alfie deposited the cooler he'd carried ashore before returning to the yacht.

Sienna turned in a circle, looking for other signs of humanity.

'Why do I get the feeling we're all alone?' she asked Emiliano.

One corner of his mouth tilted upward. 'Because we are.'

'Who owns this place?'

'I do.'

'You own two islands in the Bahamas?'

He shrugged. 'I own five, but who's counting?' Reaching into the cooler, he extracted a single item.

She lost interest in the subject of islands and rushed to the blanket. 'Oh, my God.'

He gave a low, sexy laugh. 'I thought the ice cream would capture your interest.'

She grabbed a spoon, impatiently waiting as he tore off the top of the ice-cream tub. 'I don't know how I'm going to live without these when we go back.'

Again she caught a hint of something in his eyes before it disappeared again. 'You won't have to. Everything you crave, you only have to ask for and it'll be yours.' He held out the mango-and-caramel concoction to her and she dove in.

They ate in silence until she couldn't manage another mouthful. After setting the cooler to one side, Emiliano pulled her close.

All evening, she'd been secretly terrified that he would reintroduce his no-touching policy. Relief had her melting into his arms.

'Thank you for tonight. It's been wonderful.'

'De nada, querida.'

Sensing the quiet tension in him, she raised her head to meet his eyes. 'But there's something else, isn't there?'

He nodded. 'Yes.'

A vein of apprehension threatened her bliss. 'What is it?'

'We agreed today that we both wanted the best for this child, *si*?'

She nodded a touch warily. 'Of course.'

'In that case, I think we should make the ultimate commitment.'

Her heart swan-dived from dizzying heights before taking up extreme drumming lessons against her ribs. Telling herself to keep breathing, she pulled away to look deeper into his eyes, make sure her ears weren't deceiving her.

'The ultimate commitment?'

His eyes darkened as he nodded, the flames from the lamps leaping in the gold depths as he reached into his pocket. The black velvet box bore a distinct, portentous logo. But she was more interested in the words falling from his lip. Words that made her jaw drop.

'Yes, Sienna. I'm asking you to marry me.'

CHAPTER NINE

'MARRY YOU?' SHE didn't need clarification. Not really. She just wanted to make sure she wasn't dreaming.

'Yes. Unless the idea is unsavoury to you?' The tension hadn't left his body. In fact, he was even edgier.

Sienna frowned. 'Of course not. At least, I don't think so. God, I really hate that I can't remember…'

He stared at her for a handful of seconds before he gave a decisive nod. 'Ask me what you want to know and I'll tell you.'

She rose onto her knees on the blanket and faced him. 'Have we ever discussed marriage before, even in passing?'

His jaw flexed for a second. 'No.'

Her gaze fell to the box clutched in his fist. 'So this… is really for the baby?' The drumming in her chest slowed to a dull thudding.

Emiliano's expression shuttered. 'It's for us. A united front going forward.'

'That sounds more militaristic than…'

'Than?'

She affected a careless shrug that was purely for show. 'Than I don't know… A romantic union?'

His hand dropped and his eyes narrowed. 'You've found this lacking in some way?'

Thinking about the whole evening up till now, she answered truthfully. 'No, it hasn't been lacking.' But something didn't sit right. With her memory still on vacation she didn't know how well to trust her gut. The Emiliano she could remember wasn't an openly affectionate guy, although this last week he'd shown her a different side to himself. A side she liked even more than the previous version. And, as proposals went, she was sure very little could top the magical production he'd put on for her this evening. And yet…

'You require more flowery words, perhaps?' His tone had a tight clip to it that sent a tiny shiver through her.

'Not unless they are meant, no.'

He expelled a rough breath. 'I thought we were on the same page this morning.'

'We were. We *are*. But this…'

'Your future doesn't accommodate such a commitment to me?'

'Don't put words in my mouth, Emiliano.'

He shoved his free hand through his hair. 'We are compatible in and out of the bedroom. We're dedicated to doing the best for our child. Every other obstacle can be overcome.'

Put like that, Sienna had no counterargument. Except the reality of the feelings locked within her heart. But they, like this new facet of her relationship with Emiliano, were new and untested. Didn't she owe it to herself to nurture them and see if they blossomed into something worth treasuring? Especially if her child stood to benefit, too?

Her gaze fell to the jewellery box, her heart resuming its wild hammering. Slowly, she licked her dry lips, the step she was about to take thrilling and terrifying all at once.

'Sienna?' he asked, mirroring her stance and rising onto his knees.

'What if I regain my memories and remember that you snore louder than I do?'

She expected him to laugh or shrug off her joke. But his eyes remained dark and intense. Cupping her elbows, he stared down at her for a long moment, before sliding his hands up her bare arms.

'When your memories return I hope you will give me

a chance to offer up my better qualities and plead my case on any faults you find.'

She opened her mouth, ready with an answer, because she couldn't think of any further reasons not to take the next step that promised more of everything she found enthralling about him. 'Okay.'

He seemed to stop breathing, his hands gripping her tighter as he drew closer. 'Say the words, Sienna. I need to hear you say the words.'

Swallowing, she rested her hands on his solid chest, taking strength from the heart thundering beneath her touch. 'Yes, Emiliano. I'll marry you.'

She should've known Emiliano would move with lightning speed once he had his answer. She should've known the kiss he'd delivered after she'd said yes would rock her to the foundations of her soul. She should've known the ring nestling in the box would be one of the most beautiful things she'd ever seen.

The impact of all three had her still reeling two days later as she stood in the master suite, a simple, sleeveless white gown draping her body, and two attendants who'd been ferried in from Miami fussing over how to put up her hair.

In the gardens below her bedroom, a beautiful wedding arch had been set up and a celebrant waited to perform her wedding.

Her wedding.

Emiliano's answer to her half-hearted request to wait had been, 'What for? There's no one besides Matias I wish to have at my wedding. And I am all *you* need.' The arrogant but true statement had knocked the wind out of any argument. The knowledge that he stood as a solid buffer between her and abject loneliness warmed her heart.

Enough for her to give her agreement when he'd pressed for an immediate wedding.

Now, she stared at the stunning engagement ring adorning her finger. Contrary to his denunciation of flowery words, the ring spoke volumes with its huge heart-shaped diamond and similarly shaped gems set in cascading layers on either side of the platinum band. She hadn't been able to stop staring at it since Emiliano placed it on her finger. And, within the hour, an even deeper symbol of commitment would be joining it.

She dragged her gaze from the sparkling gem and huffed beneath her breath. 'Leave it loose.'

The attendants stared at her. 'What?' the older one finally asked.

'Emiliano likes my hair loose so let's just brush it out and be done with it.' She tagged on a smile to hide her impatience.

The women exchanged glances, then they both dove into their bottomless bag of tricks and emerged clutching a delicate filigree diamond tiara.

At her nod, a hairbrush was produced and her long, black hair coaxed into a gleaming waterfall before the tiara was set into place. A touch of eye make-up and lip gloss and she was ready.

Butterflies sprouted motorised wings and beat wildly in her stomach as she descended the stairs, two long-stemmed calla lilies bound together with white velvet rope clutched in her hand. Their familiar scent calmed her a little as she walked through the living room and stepped onto the terrace, but nothing could suppress her see-sawing emotions for very long.

She was joining her life with a powerful, formidable man primarily for her baby. But she couldn't deny that she was emotionally invested, as well. And that investment seemed to be growing with each passing day. It was that knowledge that rattled her the most as she stepped onto the lawn.

One look at him and everything fell away. No, not fell away. It was more like a complete overtaking of her senses. Even from across the wide expanse of green grass, his eyes hooked on to her, holding her captive, claiming her with an implacable will that reduced all her feeble fears to nonsense.

Predatory eyes gleamed, mesmerised and pulled her close as if compelling her to the altar by his sheer will alone. Seemingly between one breath and the next she was by his side, relieved of her bouquet, ready to say the words that would join them for ever.

For ever with Emiliano Castillo.

Dressed in a dove-grey suit and a white shirt, his feet planted firmly apart, he looked larger than life... An alpha in total control of his kingdom.

Her breath shuddered out. He sent her a narrow-eyed glance then caught her hand in his. Whether his touch was meant to be reassuring or to stop her from fleeing, she wasn't sure. And she wasn't given time to dwell on it.

The celebrant was clearing his throat, his Bahamian lilt marking the start of her life-changing journey. Traditional vows were exchanged, rings slid onto fingers and blessings offered.

A deep tremble overtook her as Emiliano closed the gap between them and slid strong fingers into her hair. 'You're mine now, Sienna Castillo,' he murmured against her lips, a deep relish in his tone that escalated her trembling.

'As you are mine,' she replied, somehow noting the importance of establishing equal ownership.

'*Sí*, that is exactly so.' His voice throbbed with possessive satisfaction, binding her even more strongly than the new ring on her finger.

His mouth closed over hers, hot and demanding, uncaring that they had an audience. Over the pounding in her ears, she heard applause from the gaggle of staff and attendants. Her hands found Emiliano's waist, to hold on to and to touch him.

A mere second and an eternity later, he freed her, the feral hunger in his eyes promising the main course to the starter he'd just delivered.

Champagne was poured, a glass of sparkling mineral water handed to her, congratulations offered and received. Then she was strolling beside Emiliano along their private beach, another spectacular sunset robbing her of the breath not already captured by the man whose hand imprisoned hers.

Her husband.

His jacket had been discarded a while ago and his shirt-sleeves rolled up. Despite his casual attire, he remained a powerful, magnetically handsome force, commanding her attention with no effort at all. The sense of bewilderment snapping at her heels finally caught up with her in the form of a tiny hysterical giggle.

Emiliano stopped, his bare feet digging into the soft white sand next to hers. 'You find something amusing?'

She shook her head in wonder. 'I can't believe I'm married,' she said in a reverential whisper.

He circled round to face her, lifting her chin with a firm finger. 'Believe it. You're married. To me. And tonight I will make you mine again.'

This time her shiver was pure decadence coupled with anticipation of the highest kind. Desire flamed through her, setting the secret place between her legs alight.

She couldn't help the moan that broke free. He heard it. One corner of his mouth lifted in an arrogant smile. 'Are you ready, Sienna?'

'Sí, mi esposo,' she replied.

He jerked as if a powerful charge had jolted him. Catching her hand in his, he stalked up the beach. He stopped at the edge of the lawn and instructed her to lift her gown. Then, sinking low before her, he grabbed the water hose and washed the sand off her feet. Sienna didn't know if Emiliano's touch on her feet had ever felt this electrifying or whether the new dimension to their relationship was lending this night an extra enchantment. Whatever the reason, the urge to touch him grew too strong to contain. She slid her hand over one broad shoulder to his nape, then she snaked her fingers through his silky hair. He paused in his task, his head snapping up. Their gazes met. Meshed. Need pounded between them.

The hose was cast aside. Then he was on his feet again, tugging her after him once more.

White rose petals greeted their path when they stepped onto the terrace, and were crushed beneath their feet as they hurried down the hallway. At the foot of the stairs, Emiliano swept her into his arms. Effortlessly, he carried her into her suite. *Their* suite.

He stopped in the middle of the large, opulently decorated room. The French doors leading out to their private terrace had been pulled shut, but the last rays of sunshine streamed in, basking them in an orange-gold glow.

Letting go of her fingers, he stepped behind her. She felt a slight tug in her hair as he removed the tiara and set it aside. Moving her hair out of the way, he placed a single kiss at her nape, the breath feathering her skin and sending a delicious shiver coursing through her.

Hands drifted over her shoulders and down her arms to circle her wrists. Slowly, he lifted her arms above her head.

'Stay,' he commanded, tracing his fingers back down.

She stayed, her heartbeat frenzied, her every sense poised in wild anticipation.

He found and slid down the side zipper securing her

dréss. The satin sheath pooled at her feet, leaving her in a silk strapless bra and matching lace panties.

Behind her, his breathing altered and turned choppy.

'*Madre de Dios*, you're so beautiful.'

'I feel beautiful. Right here. With you.'

'You're beautiful, always,' he insisted. He recaptured her hands, kissing the back of one, then the other, before he let them fall to her sides. A single tug and her bra was undone and at her feet. In the next breath, Emiliano resumed his position before her, his eyes ablaze with feral hunger as his gaze moved over her.

Sliding his fingers into her hair, he planted kisses on her forehead, her eyelids, cheeks. Everywhere but where she needed him most.

Fastening her arms around his waist, she strained towards him. 'Kiss me. Please.'

He teased the corner of her mouth. 'Ask me again. In Spanish,' he ordered in a guttural voice.

'*Bésame, por favor,*' she begged.

He granted her wish and more, strong arms wrapping her in heated muscle and hot desire as he tasted, devoured and mercilessly fanned the flames of her need.

The sun had dipped beneath the horizon by the time he lifted her off her feet and placed her on the bed. Retreating, he turned on bedside lamps. Eyes never leaving hers, he deftly undid his buttons, baring his toned, bronzed chest to her everlasting delight.

Suddenly nerves overtook her. Her recollections of making love with him were a little fragmented, the memory of how *he* made her feel more sharp than the reverse. What if he found her a disappointment? Hands twisting in the sheets, she swallowed as he kicked his trousers and boxers away and prowled onto the bed.

He became absorbed in the hand he drifted down her

body, following each caress with a kiss that almost defused the troubled questions in her mind.

Almost.

Licking her lips, she cleared her throat. 'Emiliano?'

His mouth brushed against her collarbone as he answered. '*Sí, querida?*'

A moment of silence passed when words failed her.

He raised his head and frowned. 'You look troubled. Why?'

'I'm not... Show—show me...how to please you,' she stammered.

His nostrils flared with his sharp inhalation. 'You already know how. Here—' he touched his lips to her temple '—and maybe even here...' His mouth drifted down to kiss the space over her heart. 'But rest assured in the knowledge that, if you do this to me—' catching her hand, he kissed her palm then lowered it to settle over his groin, shuddering deep when she gripped his thick, impressive length '—then you're halfway there.'

He renewed his caresses, his kiss even more passionate, his strokes a touch more rough, taut cheeks flushed with arousal as he raised himself over her body. Mouth drifting over her skin, he kissed every inch, lingering over the rosy flush of her ultrasensitive nipples.

She cried out, one hand tangling in his hair to hold him there for a little while longer. Need crested high. Higher. Just when she believed she'd lose her mind if he tugged on her one more time, he freed her to continue his erotic exploration.

His hands stroked reverently over her womb, his eyes taking on a glaze of wonder as he lowered his head to place a kiss on her abdomen.

Tears she'd sworn not to shed filled her eyes. Quickly, she blinked them away, unwilling to spoil the moment. Impatient hands drew off her panties, then she was bare before his heated eyes. Parting her wider, he stroked her, growling in blatant hunger, before lowering his head to deliver the most intimate of kisses.

With his skilled tongue and deft fingers, Emiliano brought her to completion. She was still basking in delicious aftershocks when he kissed his way back up her body. She read the naked intent in his eyes, but she didn't want this to be one-sided. Raising herself onto her elbows, she nipped his firm lower lip, then used his momentary surprise to reverse their positions. His raised eyebrows nearly eroded her nerves.

But his potent scent drew her, tempted her to lower her head to his washboard torso, to attempt to deliver a fraction of the pleasure he'd just bestowed on her.

She dropped an open-mouthed kiss on his pecs. Warm and faintly salty from the sea breeze, he tasted like vitality itself. Next, she flicked her tongue over one flat nipple.

He bucked wildly against her. *'Dios mio,'* he cursed thickly.

She froze, her breath stilling with alarm. 'Did I do something wrong?'

He gave a rough groan. 'You did something right, *belleza*,' he rasped. 'So very right.'

Flush with feminine power, she repeated the caress, again and again, until not-so-steady hands bore her back onto the bed.

The eyes that met hers were the stormiest she'd ever seen. They held hers captive. Parting her thighs, he guided himself to her heated entrance.

Slowly, inch by delicious inch, absorbing her every gasp and shiver, he entered her. Fully seated inside her, he held himself there, their breaths mingling.

'Amante, you feel sublime.'

She wanted to answer. To say more. So much more. But

the indescribable feelings cascading through her robbed her of breath. That was even before he started to move.

He possessed her completely, each thrust stamping his ownership of her. Sienna could only hold on, senses and heart soaring as pleasure mounted.

She crested the wave first, but Emiliano was hard on her heels. A series of rough groans preceded hot Latin words that touched her soul and prolonged her bliss.

He was still murmuring low, deep words to her when her body cooled and she drifted off to sleep, curled up against his warmth.

Sienna wasn't sure what prompted her awake. Perhaps it was the tension vibrating off Emiliano's frame even from across the room. Or maybe it was the disturbing dreams where she'd tried repeatedly, futilely, to cling to his hand as they weathered a storm.

Whatever it was, her heart was hammering with a very different sensation from the one she'd gone to bed with when she sat up suddenly.

'What's wrong?'

He jerked around, the fingers he'd been spiking through his hair dropping to his side.

He didn't answer immediately. She got the feeling he was trying to find the right, precise words.

'Is it Matias?'

He shook his head. 'No. There's a situation in Argentina. One that I need to deal with personally.'

His parents. 'When will you return?'

Dark brows furrowed. 'Return?'

'I'm assuming you want to go on your own?'

The statement seemed to take him aback. Slowly, he walked back to bed, shedding his briefs along the way. Sliding into bed, he pulled her into his arms, tunnelling his fingers into her hair. 'On the contrary, I think it's time we faced the world. Together.'

CHAPTER TEN

THEY LEFT THE island three days later, Emiliano taking the time to make sure the information he'd received regarding Rodrigo Cabrera and his business practices was accurate. He wasn't ashamed to admit he'd deliberately delayed triple-checking his facts because, having finally allowed himself the ultimate indulgence of making love to his wife, he hadn't been in a hurry to abandon his marriage bed.

But the debt he owed his brother needed to be fulfilled. And he was done with his parents and Rodrigo Cabrera imagining they could call the shots on his and Matias's lives. They needed to be dealt with, quickly and decisively.

He ended the conference call on his private jet and re-entered the main lounge.

Sienna was curled up on the large sofa with a cashmere throw tucked around her. The book she'd been reading was propped on her chest, her delicate lashes resting against her cheeks as she slept. Disposing of the book, he took the seat next to her, his hand reaching out almost of its own accord to tuck a swathe of hair behind her ear.

For a moment, he wondered whether he'd worn her out with his lustful demands since their wedding night. Then he recalled with satisfaction her equally fervent responses.

If anyone had told him three months ago that they were capable of achieving another level of carnal intimacy, he would've dismissed it out of hand. The past three days had proved conclusively otherwise. But, while he was more than pleased with their activities in the bedroom, Emiliano was becoming aware that intimacy was creeping in elsewhere. He felt unsettled when she was out of his sight;

her laughter made his heart race in ways he couldn't quite describe.

Last night, when a nightmare had disturbed her sleep, he'd lain awake with her, talking long into the night about their hopes for their child. In the past, his conversation with Sienna had mostly circled around work and broad outside interests.

Those quiet hours together had brought a certain…contentment. One he wasn't used to. One he wasn't sure he could trust not to get in the way of logical thinking in future.

Because there was still the matter of the weeks they'd been apart to deal with when her memories returned. He might prefer this softer, more open version of Sienna, but there were no guarantees she would remain the same woman. No guarantees that her feelings would remain mutual. His child's legitimacy was safeguarded—not really necessary in this modern world, he knew, but still a firm foundation on which to build a life. And Emiliano was certain that a little foundation was better than none. Without Matias's support underpinning his own attempt at a new start in life, Emiliano wouldn't have been the man he was today.

Which meant that while he could lose himself in his wife's arms every now and then, getting used to it—or, worse, imagining he could rely on any unknown feelings she might have—was dangerous.

'You're thinking far too hard, *cariño*,' her sleep-soft voice murmured.

Despite the severe caution he'd just placed on his floundering emotions, Emiliano experienced a buzz at the effortless endearment and an even deeper thrill when sultry green eyes connected with his.

'I'm strategizing,' he replied. 'Go back to sleep.'

She made a face and sat up. 'Your game face just scared

away any notion of sleep. Tell me what you're strategizing about. Maybe I can help.'

He forced his body not to tense, and again momentarily wished he hadn't been so hasty to let her leave the insulated safety of his island. Looking away from her face, he chose his words carefully.

'My parents got themselves involved with the clichéd unsavoury businessman who was supposed to be a friend. They entered a deal with him hoping to make maximum profit with minimum output. Elite polo outfits are difficult to break into in Argentina. Rodrigo used his family friendship with my parents to gain a foothold, then cut them out, giving them the option to buy in again at a steep price. They embezzled from their own company to save themselves from bankruptcy.'

She made a disgusted sound. 'That's the definition of a recipe for disaster.'

'Exactly. My father would deny it to his last breath, of course, but he doesn't have the first clue about business. His strategy for dealing with this problem has been wrong from the very start.'

Intelligent eyes rested on him. 'But you have a way?'

'Of course. There is always a way, if you take the time to look.'

Her laugh was low, sexy, incendiary to his senses. 'I'm glad I'm not facing you across the boardroom table.'

He rose from his seat, crossed to the sofa and slid in next to her. 'It would be a delight to have you facing me. I could savour the thought of what I would do to you once I won.'

One sleek eyebrow curved upward. 'Really? By the time I *let* you win, you'd probably be too worn out to follow through.'

Something swelled in his chest, the way it did lately whenever they were immersed like this in conversation. 'Is that a challenge to my manhood?'

Faint colour tinged her cheeks as her gaze dropped to his thighs, but she tried to project an air of nonchalance. 'I'm just stating a fact. I don't need my memories to tell me I'm no slouch in the boardroom.'

He wisely conceded the argument. 'You're no slouch anywhere.'

A wide smile transformed her face. 'Thank you.'

From then, it seemed the most natural thing in the world to lean in and kiss the full, tempting mouth. And carry on kissing her until a throat cleared nearby.

He turned to find Alfie, hovering with a tray.

Sienna groaned half-heartedly. 'Between Alfie and all the cooks you have stationed at your residences, I'm going to get hopelessly fat.'

'It's a privilege to care for you while you care for our child.'

Had he not been totally absorbed by the sunlight slanting through the window onto her face, he would've missed the bruised hurt that momentarily clouded her eyes.

He frowned inwardly, wondering where he'd made a misstep. But then her gaze swept up and she was smiling at Alfie as he set out her meal.

Excusing himself, because he wanted every single cog in place before he landed in Buenos Aires, he returned to the conference area. The last time he'd flown to his homeland, he'd been woefully unprepared, and that had cost him. He didn't intend it to happen a second time.

For the next four hours, he worked. But, although his business brain sifted meticulously through facts and figures, his subconscious couldn't dismiss the look he'd seen in Sienna's eyes. His mention of the baby—had that been wrong? He didn't think so. They'd talked openly about their child. They'd talked about him. About Matias. But not about much else... Not about her.

The pen he'd been bouncing in his hand froze. Did she

feel neglected? In a bid to follow the doctor's orders—
and, yes, perhaps selfishly to keep the problem-free status
quo—was he in danger of making her feel the loneliness
she thought was behind her?

Frowning, he rose from his desk and stood at the entrance of the short galley that led to the living area. She
was still seated on the sofa, legs curled underneath her,
her book back in her hand. Beauty and sharp intelligence
shone from her face and that peculiar sensation in his chest
grew as he stared at her.

Sensing his gaze, she raised her head. Smiled.

Although the smile transformed her face, Emiliano
caught the shadows in her eyes. He wanted to tell himself it was nothing, but the fine hairs prickling his nape
told him it was something. *Something* that needed to be
dealt with.

But first, he needed to come clean. Ensure their marriage held no secrets.

Sienna was strong. Had been growing stronger still
with each passing day. They would talk things through,
he would admit his faulty choices and they would move on.

'Emiliano?' Her head was tilted and she was staring at
him with questions in her eyes.

He started towards her, then cursed under his breath
when his co-pilot emerged from the cockpit to announce
they would be landing in fifteen minutes.

Taking his seat next to her, he ensured they were both
buckled in. 'Later, *querida*. We'll talk later, when this is
all over, yes?'

Her nod was wary, the shadows under her eyes a little
more pronounced. The nightmares she'd experienced in
the last two days had clearly taken their toll. Or could it
be something else?

Yes, it was most definitely time to clear the air once and
for all. But first, he had to deal with Cabrera.

What he'd planned might take a little time, depending on how obstinate his opponent chose to be.

He planned to be quick and merciless, but he didn't intend to be in Argentina one minute longer than necessary. He had a life to live and a wife to plan it with.

The mansion in Cordoba—rarely used, according to Emiliano—had its own lake and man-made waterfall that dropped dramatically onto rocks in enthralling fashion. The orange-roofed, whitewashed residence was large enough to house several families, two additional wings having been added when he'd purchased it.

The whole property seemed to go on for acres and acres, even from the bird's-eye view of the helicopter circling to land on the manicured lawn.

'Why did you want to make it bigger?' she asked him.

To her surprise he seemed a touch embarrassed, but the look was quickly replaced by his customary self-assured shrug. 'I was newly successful and a little cocky and, yes, I wanted the world to know it. Contrary to popular belief, size does matter.'

She searched his face and saw the emotion he was trying to hide. 'You wanted your parents to finally see you, witness your success and acknowledge their shortcomings,' she offered softly, having discovered that talking with him about his past helped ease the bitterness she sometimes glimpsed in his eyes.

She also selfishly used their talks to work through her own emotions about her mother's motivation for abandoning her. She would never know the true reason, but she was beginning to accept that not everyone was cut out to accept the huge responsibility of caring for another life, even one they'd brought into the world. Emiliano's parents hadn't abandoned him, but they might as well have. That new kinship between them strengthened her even more than before. Where she'd been brave enough to face the world on her own, and thrive, it warmed her to know she didn't have to face every single obstacle on her own.

But it didn't stop her heart aching for Emiliano, for what he'd been through, every cell in her body wishing she could take his pain away.

His jaw flexed for a second before she got another shrug. 'Like I said, I was cocky. And misguided.'

'You were reaching out, the best way you knew how. Don't regret that you tried.'

His gaze searched hers for several heartbeats, before he exhaled and nodded. 'Enough about that. Come, I'll show you around.'

There was much to show. Swimming pool, stables, an internal courtyard with meticulously tended potted plants, an extensive wine cellar, countless bedrooms, a tennis court and even a tiny stone bridge over the narrowest part of the swan-inhabited lake.

To one side of the large outer patio, there was a *quincho* complete with double barbecues and roasting pits. Vintage saddles hung on the walls along with old black-and-white photos of gauchos. The wear on the saddles indicated they'd been well used at one point. Everywhere she looked, she saw evidence of past care and present attention. Emiliano hadn't bought a property to flaunt in his parents' faces, he'd invested in a potential home bursting with history.

It broke her heart that a place clearly intended to be lived in and loved had been left maintained but essentially abandoned. 'When was the last time you came here?'

'It's been two years. But Matias used it when he visited the city.'

She smiled. 'I'm glad. It feels wrong somehow for this place not to be lived in.'

He sent her a puzzled glance before leading her back

inside. Ochre tiled floors perfectly balanced white walls and arched windows.

Their suite repeated the same theme with a massive four-poster bed made of dark oak and laid with a rich, multihued spread.

Tugging her to where he stood, he began to undo the buttons of her yellow sundress. She thought about protesting that she could take care of her own undressing, but the wide yawn that overtook her put paid to that.

Once his own clothes were taken care of, she followed him into the bathroom, keeping her ogling to a few dozen stares. In the shower, she braced her hands on the wall and let him wash her, wrap her in a warm towel and lead her to bed. Her eyelids were drooping by the time he stepped back. 'Dinner will be served after you've had your rest. I'm not sure when I'll be back. Don't wait up for me.'

She nodded drowsily, the sleep that had eluded her for the past few nights determined to drag her under now. 'Go slay 'em.'

Cool arrogance glittered in his tawny eyes. 'I fully intend to,' he replied, his voice attaining an edge of steel. Bending, he touched his lips to her temple. 'Sleep well.'

She didn't.

In fact the pattern continued for nearly a week. With Emiliano fully immersed in the situation with his parents, she was left pretty much to her own devices. She would swim, visit the horses in the stables and potter around the herb garden that the housekeeper, Blanca, tended with meticulous care. All activities designed to provide the exercise she needed and, hopefully, grant her a good night's rest.

But barely an hour after going to bed she would jerk awake, sharp, dark images piercing through her subconscious and transforming into physical pain. On the seventh night in a row, she lay in the dark, her heart hammering as she tried to breathe through the ache in her head. After endless minutes, the pain began to subside.

Rising, she shrugged on a dressing gown and made her way to the kitchen. Emiliano was out at yet another meeting and the staff had retired.

Fetching a glass of water, she sipped as she wandered through the house, gratefully noting her headache had retreated to a dull throb. She eventually ended up in the inner courtyard, taking a seat before the low firepit that warmed the cool night air. When Alfie found her a few minutes later and offered to bring her a snack, she shook her head.

She had no appetite. And she was finding it increasingly difficult to shake off the sense of déjà vu crawling over her. Realising these past few days was the first time she'd been on her own without Emiliano nearby sent a jolt of alarm through her.

She'd already acknowledged that her feelings were getting troublingly intense when it came to her husband. The idea that craving him was manifesting in other ways made her heart lurch before she pursed her lips.

No. She wasn't a feeble, wilting flower unable to function without her man by her side. She didn't need to be told she'd risen to the position of a vice-president at Castillo Ventures through anything other than sheer grit and determination.

All this…anxiety bubbling beneath her skin was just a natural reaction to readjusting to the real world. Castillo Island had been a perfect, heady paradise. But not a place she could realistically stay for ever.

With that thought in mind, she rose and followed the sounds of crockery to the kitchen. Alfie turned at her entrance.

'Did you need something?' he asked.

'A pen and pad, please, if you have any handy.'

His smile widened as he opened a nearby drawer and took out the items. 'Is it time for a new list?' he asked, then he visibly checked himself. 'I'm sorry.'

She shook her head. 'Don't be. Emiliano has already told me about my list-making habits.'

She noted the relief on his face as she pulled out a stool at the kitchen island and sat down. Her first list consisted of baby names divided into male and female columns. It didn't escape her notice that the top ones were Spanish.

Next she made a list of things a baby would need.

At some point, Alfie slipped a plate of food in front of her. The grilled chicken cutlets and herb potato salad was half finished by the time she'd finished her third list.

Somewhere in the house, a clock chimed eleven o'clock. Her mind started to drift to Emiliano. Resolutely, she pulled it back.

But her husband was intent on making his presence felt despite his absence. Because on the pad in front of her, his name was written in bold letters and circled beneath it she'd written 'don't fall in love.'

She was back in bed but wide awake when she heard the crunch of tyres on gravel. Pretending she was asleep was childish and beneath her, although she did contemplate it for an absurd second.

The truth was she'd been craving elusive oblivion since her subconscious had blurted what her heart feared—that falling in love with Emiliano would be her undoing. Her panic that it may already be too late, that she was in all probability more than halfway there, was what had kept her body poised on the brink of full-blown panic.

Footsteps approached. She sat up, an intrinsic vein of courage stopping her from cowering away from her fears.

Emiliano entered and froze at the sight of her. For a few charged seconds, he stared at her, then a slow smile curved his mouth, the palpable tension blanketing him easing a touch.

'I meant it when I said don't wait up. But I do like the idea of you waiting up in bed for me.'

Despite his easy words, grim lines bracketed his mouth. Gleefully pushing aside her own disturbing emotions, she focused on his.

'Did everything go according to plan?'

The muscles in his neck bunched as he tossed his head in a purely Latin motion of vexation. 'Cards were laid on the table. A few threats tossed in. I expect compliance to be forthcoming in the next twelve hours.'

'How did you do it?' she asked. She'd been probing him on the subject since they arrived, but he'd remained tight-lipped about his dealings.

He hesitated for a moment then he prowled forward, shrugging off his jacket and discarding it on a scrolled seat. The innate sexiness of his every movement dried her mouth and spiked her heartbeat. It was all she could do not to lunge for him when he dropped onto the bed and slid one hand over her thigh.

'Men like Cabrera operate on greed and tend to spread themselves thin in the hope of making multiple paydays at any one time. I targeted his most lucrative companies and convinced a few key shareholders to part with their shares for a considerable markup. Then it was just a matter of making it clear that I would take pleasure in making his life hell if he didn't leave Castillo Estate alone.'

'Wow.'

He rubbed his free hand over his growing stubble. '*Sí*. Wow.'

She frowned. 'You don't wear victory well,' she commented.

'I'm dealing with a slippery bastard. I won't celebrate until the ink is dry on our new agreement.' His hand reached her hip and circled sensuously before continuing its path of destruction. The unique scent of sandalwood and alpha male invaded her senses.

She forced herself not to lean in, not to abandon cheerfully all her caution for this man. But the sensation of being on a slippery slope escalated. So she covered deep disquiet with more conversation. 'Nevertheless, you should allow yourself a moment of satisfaction for progressing this far, this quickly.'

His mouth pursed. 'The prospect of spending time with my parents kills my celebratory spirit.'

'Spending time…?'

'I went to deliver the news of their…impending freedom…and to discuss Matias. They refused to talk about it tonight.'

'Have you considered that they're scared?'

'Being scared is acceptable. Burying their heads in the sand and refusing to even discuss it is not,' he stated. 'They wish to sleep on it before making their decision. They will give me an answer when they come to dinner tomorrow.'

Her eyes widened. 'They're coming here?'

He nodded grimly.

'If you're this unhappy about it, why did you agree to it?'

The corners of his mouth turned down. 'My happiness doesn't matter in this. I agreed for Matias.'

'Why a meal, though?'

He eyed her for a long second. 'Matias isn't the only reason for their request. They also want to meet you.'

Her mouth dropped open. 'Me? Why?' she blurted.

His gaze swept down for a handful of seconds. 'To satisfy whatever curiosity keeps them from facing reality, I guess.'

'Do they…do they know about the baby and my accident?'

His lip pursed. 'They know you're recovering from a trauma, but I didn't see the need to tell them about the baby. They were never interested in their son. I don't wish for them to have any interest in a grandchild.'

His tone was firm. Bitter. Punctuated with definitive finality as he dragged her lower and climbed on top of her.

Lowering his head, he brushed his mouth over hers in a whisper-thin caress. 'Since you seem rested and were considerate enough to wait up for me, *belleza*, I think we shouldn't let this opportunity go to waste, hmm?'

Every single pre-emptive she'd mentally erected crumbled to dust the moment he slid his tongue across her lower lip. As her hands found their way to his shoulders, she told herself she would take up arms to safeguard her feelings again tomorrow.

Tonight, she needed to experience her husband's love-making one more time.

CHAPTER ELEVEN

'YOU'RE MAKING A LIST?'

She heard the trace of amusement in Emiliano's voice a second before he dropped a kiss on her head.

'If you were given less than a day's notice to host your first ever in-laws' dinner, you would make a list, too. Don't scoff.'

His amusement disappeared. 'They are not your in-laws, except in name only. And don't fret about it. Alfie and Blanca will take care of everything.'

She looked out through the open doors of the kitchen to the courtyard where Alfie was hosing down the tiles. 'He has his hands full. Besides, keeping *my* hands full will stop me fretting.'

Emiliano's eyes glittered with the beginning of displeasure. 'Sienna...'

'It's done, Emiliano. The driver's taking Blanca and me into town in half an hour. She does the grocery shopping and I get to practise my Spanish. It's a win-win.'

'I disagree. You can stay at home instead, go for a swim, practise your Spanish on me. Win-win-win.'

She'd woken up this morning with a sense of dread hanging over her. She couldn't deny that a large part of it stemmed from last night and how fast she'd succumbed to the magic of being in Emiliano's arms. And, whichever way she tried to dress it up, she wasn't looking forward to meeting Emiliano's parents, knowing they had deliberately rejected one son while being cavalier with the other's health. Before she'd sat down to start a fresh list, she knew she needed some distance. And she was going to take it, regardless of the fumes of ire vibrating off the sleekly built man standing before her.

'It's a tempting offer, but I'm still going, Emiliano,' she stated firmly.

His jaw flexed with irritation. 'I'm beginning to think I should've booked a restaurant for tonight and been done with it.'

She hopped from the island counter, quickly dancing out of his reach when his hands started to move towards her.

Yes. Distance. Definitely.

Steady footsteps approached the kitchen and she looked up, relief spiking through her as the housekeeper entered. 'Well, it's too late now.' She started to walk out.

'Wait.' The bite in his tone was definitely growing.

She stopped, her nerves jangling as he strolled towards her. He hadn't yet shaved his stubble from last night and, with the predatory gleam in his eyes, he resembled a dark overlord intent on one thing only: establishing claim.

'Bésame adiós,' he ordered in a near growl.

There was no getting away from the demand. Not if she wanted to escape. Inhaling deeply, she rose on tiptoe and pressed her mouth against his. Hard. Quick.

She started to turn away.

One hand captured her nape, the other cupping her jaw, totally halting her retreat. Incisive eyes narrowed, he bared his teeth. 'Once again, with feeling.'

Sienna was at once elated and terrified by how high her senses leaped. So much so, she stood immobile as he slanted his mouth over hers and kissed her in a way that left little room for doubt that she was well and truly owned, her heart unmistakably on the line.

When he raised his head, she was panting. And his eyes gleamed with arrogant satisfaction. She stared dumbly when he held a granite-black credit card in front of her face between two fingers, before reaching behind her to tuck it into the pocket of her white capri trousers.

'Enjoy your shopping,' he rasped. 'And Alfie comes with you. Non-negotiable.'

Sienna stumbled away, barely noting the drive out of the villa or the expansive *pampas* that whizzed by her window.

Time passed. She wasn't sure how long. Alfie, in the passenger seat, glanced back at her, his gaze concerned. 'Everything all right, Sienna?'

She attempted a reassuring smile that failed completely. Because she wasn't all right. With one kiss, one final blow against her poorly erected defences, the truth had been laid bare.

She was in love with Emiliano. Irrevocably. Completely.

Her senses flared wide, utterly vulnerable at that silent, devastating admission.

Had it been heading there since that first admission of her deeper feelings on that forgotten trip to Hong Kong? Had it grown even more during the months now buried in the darkness of her memories?

Did he know how she felt?

Recalling the look she'd caught on his face on the plane yesterday, her heart dropped in further alarm. Was that why he wanted to talk?

'Sienna?'

Pushing the tsunami of questions away to be dealt with later, she summoned a smile. 'I'm fine.'

You hope.

Refusing to grant victory to the inner voice that mocked, she raised her chin. Yes. She hoped. When she'd bravely stepped up to the altar and said her vows, it'd been because she wanted this union to work. For her baby and for herself.

If the father of her child didn't want the love that blossomed in her heart for him, then…then…

Her breath shortened, actual physical pain lancing

through her head, as if the thought was dead against being formed. She gasped.

Over the buzzing in her ears she heard Alfie instructing the driver to pull over. 'No, it's okay. I'm okay.'

She would be. For her baby's sake, she had to be.

Letting that vow strengthen her, she resolutely shut off her thoughts, focusing on her first glimpse of the more urban parts of Cordoba. Like every other cosmopolitan metropolis, it contained flashy new buildings. But it was the more traditional architecture that she watched out for. Beside her, Blanca proudly pointed out pale gold stone churches, piazzas teeming with tourists splashing through fountains and Manzana Jesuitica, a UNESCO World Heritage site.

She smiled and nodded, aware of Alfie's frequent sidelong glances. It was almost a relief to arrive at the bustling square that was Cordoba's main produce market and lose herself in the sights and smells of Argentina.

Cured meats and Wagyu beef were chosen and expertly sliced... Wild pink salmon was carefully packaged and added to the ever-growing pile. Plump fruit and fresh vegetables were placed in cool boxes to protect them from the growing heat and, all too soon, they were piling back into the SUV.

But they only went a few streets before the driver was pulling to a stop once more.

'Why are stopping? Did we forget something?' she asked.

Alfie grinned. 'Yes, proper retail therapy for you. Boss's orders.'

She took a closer look at the street and shops in front of which they were parked: expensive cars and chic boutiques which reeked of exclusivity. Alfie got out and held her door open. Blanca smiled and waved her out with expressive hands.

A little relieved at the reprieve she'd been given before facing Emiliano again with the new knowledge burning in her heart, Sienna alighted and entered the nearest shop.

The staff was busy bustling around two women holding court at one end of the shop. One harried server offered her champagne, a look of relief crossing her face when Sienna refused. A second later, she darted off.

Not minding the peace, she took her time to browse. Her pregnancy wasn't overly visible yet, but she'd noticed a definite thickening of her waistline and a general tightness in her clothes. The chance to outfit herself with a confidence-boosting dress was suddenly welcome.

The drop-sleeve gown she found was a floaty, gossamer-light affair. In dark, layered purple, it was elegant enough to wear to dinner and loose enough to disguise her slight bump. The price tag however was staggering enough to give her pause.

'The dressing room is that way,' Alfie said. 'Here, I'll help you.' He took the dress from her and firmly led the way, as if he could sense her hesitation.

The harassed server approached them again and showed them to the large changing room before hurrying off once more. Alfie rolled his eyes, but grinned as he nudged her towards the wide cubicle.

The dress fitted like a dream, but she was still biting her lip about the price as she changed into her clothes and emerged from the changing room to hear raised voices.

'*Sí*, Señora Castillo. *Immediatamente!*'

Sienna frowned. She didn't know how common the Castillo name was in this part of Argentina but what were the chances of coming across another one in Cordoba?

The older woman was still on a diva tirade. Alfie rolled his eyes when his gaze met hers. Deciding to buy the dress and leave as quickly as possible, she took the credit card out of her back pocket.

About to dismiss the scene, she froze when a younger voice joined in the haranguing.

'*Lo siento*, Señorita Cabrera,' one of the assistants offered.

The rest of the rapid-fire words were lost to Sienna as the fine hairs on her nape jerked upright. It would be a coincidence that the two names behind the reason for her being in Argentina belonged to random strangers.

Slowly, she emerged from the changing area, her attention on the two women seated behind the roped-off VIP area, each clutching a chilled glance of champagne in one hand and gesticulating to distraught assistants with the other.

The younger woman spotted Sienna first. Her dark brown gaze drifted over. Paused. Returned. Widened.

She turned, nudged the older woman and muttered under her breath. Then both glanced her way, eyes filled with curiosity.

The older woman rose first. Tall and willowy, she only needed to take a couple of steps towards her before Sienna became certain that she was looking at Emiliano's mother. They had the same eyes. The same curve of her lip. But, where Emiliano's regal posture and innate grace of movement was absorbingly effortless, everything about Señora Castillo seemed affected, right down to the tips of her manicured fake nails.

'Your name?'

Sienna blinked. 'Excuse me?'

She gave an uppity sniff as her gaze raked over Sienna. 'I am Valentina Castillo. My friend seems to think we might have a person of interest in common. I merely wish to ascertain if this is correct.' Her tone was clipped, the bites of heavily accented English supposed to give an impression of class. Sienna could only concentrate on the words that had just come out of her mouth.

Her friend? *'Person of interest?'*

The younger woman joined them, the swing in her shorter, voluptuous hips more natural. Up close, Sienna couldn't help but notice her stunning beauty. And the fact that something about her made her senses tweak in alarm even though, at closer scrutiny, her expression was more welcoming than Valentina's.

'You are Sienna Newman, *si*?' she asked in a soft, husky voice, her eyes now transmitting friendliness.

Sienna smiled. 'Sienna Castillo,' she corrected.

The women exchanged glances then stared back at her. From the corner of her eye, Sienna noted Alfie's concerned frown but she concentrated on Emiliano's mother, desperately probing for a sign of warmth or humanity. Coming up empty, she took a breath and attempted a smile regardless. 'If by *person of interest* you mean Emiliano, then, yes, we do. It's lovely to make your acquaintance, Señora Castillo.'

'That remains to be seen, my dear.' Her gaze dropped to the dress in Sienna's hand, then to the credit card. She couldn't have failed to see Emiliano's name embossed in gold letters. A look lanced through her eyes, even as one carefully plucked eyebrow rose.

Sienna wanted to shove the card back in her pocket, but she forced herself to remain still. She had nothing to be ashamed of. All the same, she made a mental note to find out where her own bank cards were when she got back.

Valentina dismissed her but, just before she turned away, Sienna also spotted something in the woman's gaze. Fear.

'We will see you this evening. I hope you don't feel too out of your depth catering for our particular tastes.'

'Your son prides himself in having the best of everything. Don't worry, we have you covered.'

Sienna witnessed the tiniest grimace tweak her mother-in-law's features before a stiff smile slid into place. 'In that case, we look forward to making your better acquaintance, as you say. *Vamanos*, Graciela.' Her gentle tone as she addressed the younger woman spoke of a fondness.

Graciela Cabrera trailed behind the older woman, then at the last moment before they reached the door she darted back.

'I hope we meet again, but if we don't you should know that Emiliano is a wonderful man. One you should treasure.'

Sienna's mouth dropped open. 'I… Thank you.'

Graciela nodded, her eyes staying on Sienna's a moment longer before she turned and quickly walked out.

'Um… What was that all about?' Alfie enquired.

'I have no idea,' she murmured a split second before she experienced that twinge again, sharper this time. But the pain of her burgeoning headache was nowhere near the ache she felt in her heart for Emiliano. She hadn't wanted to believe that a mother could be so unfeeling. Having met Valentina Castillo, Sienna was willing to bet the woman's demeanour was a front. She might have taken a wrong path in the past where her second child was concerned, but the need she'd glimpsed ever so briefly in her eyes gave Sienna a little hope for her husband.

As for Graciela…

She frowned, touching a hand to her temple when the jumbled thoughts made her head pound harder.

'What do you say we get out of here?' Alfie suggested.

'Yes, good idea,' she replied.

The assistants, chattering quietly and looking relieved now that the drama queens had exited, came forward and rang up the dress.

Sienna got back into the SUV, feeling as if her life had changed but unable to put her finger on how.

Like the outbound journey, the return trip went by in a blur. The first thing she knew about being back at the estate was Emiliano bearing down on her, his face a mask of displeasure.

'I understand you met my mother,' he growled, taking her hands in his and peering down at her with dark, searching eyes.

'I had the pleasure, yes. Graciela Cabrera was there, too.'

He stiffened, his body taking on a grim alertness that twanged her already jangled nerves. 'What did she say?' he bit out.

'Graciela? She was nice. Your mother...' She paused, unwilling to pass negative judgement on the woman, especially when her beliefs about Valentina had grown stronger. Somewhere deep in her heart, she still harboured hope that his parents would wake up to the incredible, arrogant man who so easily held the world in his hand. The stunningly charismatic man she'd fallen in love with.

The reality of her ever-growing feelings rammed home just then. So powerfully that she couldn't stare into his eyes for fear he would decipher her emotions. Drawing her hands from his, she waved the question away. 'It's fine. She was probably as surprised as I was to meet me this way.'

He huffed with annoyance. 'I am one hundred per cent certain it is not fine, and you do not need to make excuses for her, but in the spirit of peace I will leave the subject alone.'

'Thank you,' she murmured. Then, eager to escape, because the temptation to stay was mounting by the second, she turned towards the kitchen. 'Blanca probably needs help—'

'No.' Emiliano's mouth thinned, despite the proffered peace. 'Blanca has assistants who have minions. You're officially barred from the kitchen until further notice.'

'But—'

'Let's not argue a pointless issue, *querida*. Come.' Without waiting for her consent, he caught her elbow, steered her into the living room and pressed her onto the wide sofa. Encouraging her to lie back, he eased her shoes off and propped her feet in his lap.

Sienna gave up attempting to find fortitude in the storm of domineering attitude. Just as she couldn't help greedily drinking him in, or stop the heat dredging through her pelvis at his dark, devastating looks. When his thumbs dug into her soles with pinpoint accuracy, she closed her eyes and moaned, surrendering to his touch.

'Cancelling tonight seems like a better prospect by the second,' he rasped.

Her eyes popped open. 'No, don't cancel. Your mother will think it's my fault.'

'I don't care what she thinks. Neither should you.'

She shook her head, hope still burning in her chest. 'But you do care how it might affect Matias. Once they satisfy their curiosity, they won't have a leg to stand on.'

He sighed, his jaw flexing for a second before he jerked out a nod. They stayed like that, Emiliano massaging her feet, Sienna desperately biting her tongue to stop the thick, emotive words that surged forth.

Because, really, what was the worst that could happen?

He could reject you. Reject your love.

Chains tightened around her heart, which in turn robbed her of breath and silenced the words.

When he rose an hour later and held out his hand to her, she went with him upstairs to their bedroom. The impending dinner ominously had taken up room in their minds, which left very little room for banter as they undressed and got into the shower. Emiliano made no move to make love to her, much to her soul's mournful surprise. Telling herself it was for the best, and hearing the silent words ring hollow, she busied herself with getting ready.

Still in silence, they came downstairs and walked

through the house with the sound of last-minute preparations signalling his parents' imminent arrival.

He stood tall and proud next to her but she nevertheless felt him tense when headlights travelled slowly up the long drive. Even after the Mercedes stopped, his parents didn't alight for a full minute. Anger slowly building inside her on his behalf, Sienna linked her fingers with Emiliano's. His jaw tightened, but he didn't look at her, his focus unmoving on the idling vehicle.

When it opened and a man stepped out, her eyes widened.

She'd imagined she would be meeting a male version of Valentina. But the man who slowly walked up the steps and shook her hand appeared less…rigid. She even dared to consider that there was a malleable side to Benito Castillo as his eyes lingered on his son during their handshake.

Nevertheless, as he stepped back formally to introduce his wife, it was clear the two presented a united front.

It was also clear Valentina hadn't shared the fact that she and Sienna had already met with her husband. The knowledge wasn't worth puzzling over. The objective tonight was to wine, dine and somehow persuade Valentina and Benito Castillo to do the right thing by their older son sooner rather than later.

So she followed Emiliano into the living room where Alfie was waiting to prepare drinks.

While the men opted for scotch and Valentina a glass of white wine, she chose a lemon spritzer. They indulged in stilted conversation for interminable minutes before her mother-in-law's gaze settled on her. 'That dress suits you. You look…radiant.'

Beside her, she felt Emiliano's tension mount but she kept the smile pinned on her face. 'Thank you. Allow me to return the compliment.'

Valentina looked startled for a moment at being called

radiant, then her gaze skittered to her son. And, just like her husband's had, it lingered.

Sienna breathed easier, not sure how they would navigate themselves out of the quagmire but choosing to believe they would.

After a minute, Benito cleared his throat. 'About this business with Cabrera…'

'It's been taken care of. As of this afternoon, he will no longer be a problem. Castillo Estate is back under full Castillo care.'

A wave of relief washed over his parents' faces, although Valentina's mouth pursed. 'You have our undying gratitude, of course, but I can't help but think all this… unpleasantness could've been avoided if you'd honoured your word at the start.'

Emiliano inhaled sharply, his eyes darting to Sienna's before narrowing with vicious intent on his mother. 'I understand that gratitude is an alien concept to you, but we will *not* discuss subjects that are in the past.'

Valentina drank more wine and waved a compliant hand. 'Of course, I understand. Now that you're married, it would be distasteful of me to bring it up.'

Sienna's heart lurched. The glass in her hand shook wildly, spilling several drops of liquid on her dress. Thin-lipped and a little paler than he'd been a moment ago, Emiliano reached into his pocket and passed her a handkerchief.

She took it, but she was nowhere near interested in the stains on her dress. 'What…what does that mean?' she asked, the dread that had been haunting her growing exponentially.

'It means that whatever insane ideas they entertained to extricate themselves from their situation is no longer worth discussing, since Cabrera is no long an issue. *Está claro?*' The warning in his tone was deadly.

Enough to convince her there was more going on beneath the surface. Enough to tell her he'd just given her a non-answer.

Eyes a shade darker than her son's snapped. 'We are your parents, Emiliano. Show some respect!'

Emiliano surged to his feet. 'I will not be dictated to under my own roof. Perhaps you misunderstood what I meant when I said Castillo Estate was back in Castillo care. What I meant is it's back in *my* care. Part of my agreement with Cabrera was that he sells me all his shares. As of this afternoon, I own seventy-five per cent of the business. I will oversee the business from now until Matias is back at the helm. Then I will transfer control to him.'

Both Benito and Valentina wore equal expressions of astonishment. Valentina recovered first, a touch of anguish mingled with her shock. 'You would do that to us?'

'It's already done.' His merciless gaze flitted to the door leading to the dining room, where Alfie hovered. 'I believe dinner is served. While we eat, you will tell me when you will be instructing the doctors in Switzerland to bring my brother out of his coma,' he spat at his mother. 'But, make no mistake, by the time dessert is served I will have your agreement. Or you can kiss your precious estate goodbye.'

Dinner was a disaster. Fraught silence was followed by sniping between Valentina and Benito, followed by an increasingly circumspect Benito. Every now and then, his gaze landed on his son, his expression slowly changing from brooding to acceptance and eventually to grudging respect.

Emiliano finally laid down his fork. 'Is there something on your mind?'

Benito shrugged and picked up his replenished glass of red wine. '*Sí*. We wouldn't be in this mess if it weren't for your mother's obsession with the Cabreras. A habit I indulged unfortunately. We're lucky enough to have salvaged our family name. So we will do everything you want. And when Matias is back he will manage the Castillo business, with no interference from us.'

Valentina's gasp was followed by hot Spanish words exchanged with her husband, who shrugged some more and drank even harder. When she realised her tirade had lost its legs, she shifted her gaze to her son. 'I… We will do as your father says. And, for what it's worth, you should know we talked to Matias's doctors this morning. They are…hopeful.'

'Good, then everything is resolved.'

Valentina's expression dropped, her eyes displaying a greater depth of anguish than before.

Sienna glanced at Emiliano, curious as to how he was taking this turn of events. He wasn't looking at his parents. His eyes rested on her, their expression intently watchful. Almost dreading.

A shiver went over her as terror crept closer to her heart.

Throwing down her napkin, she stood. 'I'll go and see about dessert.' The ungracious voice that said she was up for anything that hurried this overwrought meal to its conclusion was ruthlessly silenced as she entered the kitchen.

Blanca had everything under control, of course.

Feeling superfluous and unwilling to return to the warped atmosphere of the dining room, Sienna carried on walking through the kitchen, stepping out into the outer courtyard. Inhaling the fresh, clean air did nothing for her raging thoughts and the almost fatalistic, dreadful premonition haunting her.

Footsteps sounded behind her, a click of heels bringing certain doom.

Sienna turned.

Valentina stood six feet away, her gaze resting on Sienna's stomach. 'Is that how you got him to go back on his word? By getting yourself pregnant? And don't bother denying it. Your abstention from drink and Emiliano watching you like a hawk tells me what I need to know.'

'I don't know what you mean. Go back on his word on what?' she asked through lips turning numb with fear.

'Ah, of course, you don't remember.'

'Don't remember what?' she probed again.

Valentina turned, as if she was about to walk away. 'It doesn't matter now that he's married, I suspect.'

'You do care for him. So why do you treat him like that? Why are you so afraid to show it?' Sienna blurted before she thought better of it.

Valentina's eyes widened. 'You don't know what you're talking about. I don't treat Emiliano in any particular way.'

'When was the last time you told him you loved him, or that you were proud of him?'

'He doesn't need that from me. The bond we share is enough.'

'Really? Well, I wouldn't know about that. I grew up without a mother, you see.'

'Is that supposed to make me feel sorry for you?'

Sienna stared at the older woman for a moment before she shook her head. 'No, but take it from me—your son needs to hear it from you.'

'Don't presume to think you know me enough to lecture me.'

'Very well. Please tell me what you meant by what you said before. "Now that he's married"?'

She spread her hands in a gesture so reminiscent of Emiliano's it was unsettling. 'I've been forbidden from talking about it.'

Her fists balled. 'Not by me.'

Her eyebrows rose. 'You have a backbone. You will need it to deal with my son. But are you sure it's strong enough to handle the truth?'

'What truth? Tell me,' she insisted, her voice rising with a touch of hysteria.

'Very well. A couple of months ago Emiliano was engaged to Graciela Cabrera. Their wedding had been planned for next month, on Valentine's Day. Benito thinks I'm obsessed but I only want what's best for both my sons. Graciela would've made him a good wife.'

'That's…that's a lie.' Her voice was bled of all substance.

Valentina's eyes, so similar to those of the man Sienna loved, narrowed. 'If you don't believe me, *ask him*.'

She didn't need to. Because she knew. Even before Graciela's words to her in the shop that had spoken of something else… Even before Emiliano's proposal that hadn't quite sat right… Deep in her heart, she *knew*.

Sienna opened her mouth to speak. Then quickly shut it, her hands flying to her head as every single twinge, tweak, dread and fear coalesced at the same time into a bolt of lightning that forked through her brain.

She stumbled forward, her hand flailing out in search of something, anything, to hold on to. Another arrow of pain cracked through her head. She cried out as the edges of her vision blurred.

Her baby. *Oh, God, her baby!*

Powerful feet thundered towards her, hands catching her as she lost feeling in her legs.

'*Madre de Dios*, what did you do to her?' was the last thing she heard.

She woke on the sofa to find Emiliano on his knees beside her, his face a grey mask as he gripped her hand. His breathing was hopelessly ragged, his eyes black, haunted pools.

'Sienna.' His voice was a hoarse, desperate plea.

She couldn't look at him. It simply hurt too much. So she directed her gaze over his shoulder to the heated argument going on between Valentina and Benito.

'Basta!' Emiliano snarled. 'My wife is like this because of you. Alfie will show you out. You're no longer welcome here.'

The bubble of pain bloomed as she shook her head.

'You're wrong. They had nothing to do with it. I remember, Emiliano. I remember everything. And this... *this was all because of you.'*

CHAPTER TWELVE

'WE NEED TO talk about this, Sienna.'

Three days had passed since her memory had returned. Since the sheer depths of Emiliano's cunning betrayal had shredded her heart to a million pieces.

Concern for her baby had made her agree to see the doctor Emiliano had summoned, the same concern keeping her confined to rest for three days when every screaming atom of her being wished she was elsewhere. Far away from here. From Emiliano.

God, just thinking about him hurt more than she would ever have thought possible. And having him here in her bedroom, speaking to her...

She took a deep breath and turned from the window to face him. Better to get this over with then she could go back to staring at the devastation that was her life.

Her face must have reflected the true depths of her wretchedness because he inhaled sharply. 'You need to be in bed.'

'I need to be several thousand miles from here. Away from you.'

His jaw clenched hard, as did the hands by his side. But he didn't leave as she wanted him to. He stayed put. Immovable. She found it overwhelmingly brutal just taking every breath.

'This isn't productive.'

'Productive? I'm sorry that regaining my memories to discover the man who dumped me for another woman has lied and manipulated me into marriage because he got me pregnant isn't *productive* for you.'

The doctor from Haven North with whom they'd videoconferenced had mentioned that more of her memories would return with each passing day. Sienna desperately prayed they didn't. With each new memory revealed, her heart broke all over again.

'I didn't lie to you. I just couldn't tell you the whole truth because it might have caused irreparable damage.'

'You twisted the situation to suit your own needs!'

'What needs? The need to ensure my brother didn't remain on a breathing tube for the rest of his life? Or the need to provide for my child's future?'

Her hand flew to her stomach, the thought that she would want less for her child ramping up her anger and misery. 'This child will want for nothing and I resent your implication otherwise. As for Matias, I get that you made a promise to him that you had to keep. What I can't live with is that you didn't see fit to tell me about it. You went ahead and made plans *for your life* that didn't take our relationship into account. Plans that involved another woman. Plans that were splashed all over the tabloids for the world to see and salivate over.'

'I never intended to marry her. But she asked for my help in dealing with her father—'

'I don't care! You knowingly put yourself in a position that would hurt me. And, when I tried to talk to you about it, you walked away.'

'Because you weren't in a state to listen to what I had to say.'

'Which was what? That, when it came right down to it, I featured very low on your list of priorities?'

His hand slashed through the air. 'I don't want to hear about lists!'

'I'm sorry if what's important to me doesn't coincide with what matters to you!' she snapped.

'*Dios mío*, I was hit with an unexpected situation on

what was supposed to be a turnaround visit. I had very little time to act.'

'You've made tougher decisions in a boardroom full of intransigent negotiators in a matter of hours. You were in Argentina for *six days*. And not once during that time did you call to tell me what was going on.'

'How would you have reacted if I'd called and told you that my brother had left me a message on what he thought was his possible deathbed to tell me to honour a ludicrous promise he'd made to get my parents out of their mess? That I was expected to hand myself over like a prized stud in some deal I wasn't aware of until I walked into my parents' house?'

She floundered for a second before she firmed her spine. 'I guess we'll never know, because you didn't.'

'I didn't because it was an absurd situation. One that I couldn't find an immediate solution to that didn't involve letting Matias down.'

'So you chose to let *me* down instead?'

'No. I chose to wait until we were together to tell you but…'

'But what?'

'I put myself in your shoes, considered how I would feel if you informed me you were engaged to another man.'

She stared at him, perverse curiosity eating at her. 'And?'

The feral growl that erupted from his throat startled her. She watched him spike a hand through his hair and pace for a minute before facing her. 'It was your birthday. I wanted you to enjoy your evening so I decided to wait till the next day to explain the situation. But the tabloid spread put a wrench in that.'

'So you thought the best solution then was to break up with me?'

'I thought I'd give us both a little space to regroup and for me to find an alternative solution.'

'And that involved trying to buy me with the penthouse and a car?'

He shrugged and she noted absently that his face was creased in lines that resembled anxiety. 'It was wrong, perhaps, but I wanted to keep you sweet while dealing with Rodrigo Cabrera. And I knew you loved the penthouse.'

'Not enough to live in it after it was clear we were over.'

'We weren't over. We're not over,' he denied through clenched teeth. 'We will *never* be over.'

She shook her head. 'You know what all of this tells me? That you were more concerned with everyone else's feelings than mine. And right now you're only here out of guilt and because I'm carrying your baby.'

'*Dios mío*, be reasonable.'

'No! You had weeks to fight for me. You didn't bother. I've seen you go after deals with more aggression simply because you were bored. How do you think it makes me feel to know I didn't even warrant a *bored* chase?'

His teeth bared. 'Because a large part of that time, you'd disappeared off the face of the earth. Then you had the audacity to turn up with another man whose presence in your life you rubbed in my face.'

She flushed, then felt a snap of irritation for feeling guilty. 'Don't turn this back on me. We are where we are today because of you. I don't hate you for trying to do right by your brother, but you didn't need to cast me aside to do so. Rejection like that isn't easy for me to forgive, Emiliano.' She stopped then regrouped when her voice broke. 'You know what it feels like to come second, to be discarded like an unwanted object. I may be strong enough to withstand it, but that doesn't mean I wish it to happen to me. I…I just can't come second in anyone's life. Ever again.'

He froze, the only movement in his whole formidable frame the eyes that narrowed with laser-like intent on her. 'What are you saying?' he asked in a clipped tone.

'I'm saying that I can never be sure that you're not here in this marriage just because of our child.'

'I'm here for you both!'

'But would you have asked me to marry you if I wasn't pregnant? Or was this whole thing staged to protect your position in your child's life?'

His mouth thinned and his nostrils flared. 'Nothing was staged. We're having a baby together. It's the most natural thing in the world for couples to take the next step.'

'Even when one of the couple has previously made it perfectly clear that marriage doesn't feature anywhere on his life's to-do list?'

He stalked in a tight circle before facing her again. 'I'm trying to do right by you, Sienna. Will you condemn me for that?'

Her heart lurched then broke. 'No, but I won't let you sacrifice yourself for me.'

'*Por el amor de Dios!* It is *not* a sacrifice.'

She took one step back. Then another. To stay here was to weaken and she would hate herself for it one day. The thought of what that would do to her child firmed her resolve.

'Call it what you will. But I don't want it.'

He stared at her with something akin to shock. Which turned to disbelief then cold determination. 'You don't want it. Explain to me in clear terms what you *do* want, then,' he demanded hoarsely.

Before she gave birth to the words, they burned like acid in her chest. But she had to speak them. Continuing to perpetuate a lie would kill what remained of her heart. Staying, knowing Emiliano wasn't in it for love, for *her*, would annihilate her soul. 'It means I want a divorce.'

Tawny eyes turned an eerie dark gold, the lines around his mouth deepening as his face hardened into a terrifying mask. 'I'm not prepared to dissolve our marriage over a simple disagreement.'

'It's not simple to me. I married you without the benefit of remembering that you hurt me deeply, Emiliano. And I can't trust that you won't do it again.' Not with what was most important to her besides her baby. Not with the feelings that were screaming under the weight of her hurt.

His face had lost a healthy dose of colour but the eyes that were locked onto her were dark pools of grim purpose. 'Be that as it may, my responsibility is to our child. We will not break up because you feel aggrieved. We once were in agreement that we would give this child the best of ourselves. That hasn't changed.'

'How can we do that when we're locked in battle?'

He spread his hands out in a gesture she would've been foolish to believe was harmless. 'You're the only one armed to the teeth here, *querida*. I'm just telling you where my hard boundaries are. We can work together to find common ground or you can attempt to take shots at me. Before you do, I should warn you that you will lose.'

'You can't force me to stay. Just as you can't keep what you never truly had.'

He looked stricken, as though he'd been gut-punched. His nostrils flared as he took rough, deep breaths.

Then, without another word, he walked out.

She'd come full circle. Her hand crept over her stomach. Fuller circle.

Sienna stared despondently around the flat she'd rented and tried to decorate but felt alien. Despite being back for almost two weeks and barely having left the flat, it still felt as if she was living in a stranger's property. A stranger who moved listlessly through the three rooms, eating for her child's sake and doing very little else.

In a way it was good that she hadn't grown attached to this flat. Having a baby who would quickly grow into an active toddler meant she would need a house with a garden. Somewhere more child-friendly where she could establish roots.

Her bump was definitely more rounded. Time was marching on whether she chose to acknowledge it or not. She only wished she could breathe, eat and sleep without the raw pain that dogged her whenever she thought of Emiliano.

Which was constantly.

How could she fall in love with the same man twice in one lifetime—and both times have her heart torn to pieces?

After their row in the bedroom, Emiliano had given her a wide berth for the rest of the day. When she'd requested dinner in her room, Alfie had delivered it.

The next morning, deciding it was a good time to start reclaiming her life, she'd come down to breakfast and been confronted with a grim-faced Emiliano. He'd stated with point-blank finality that he wouldn't discuss a divorce.

They'd compromised on a separation. And once again he'd walked away from her, but this time with a look that closely resembled fierce anguish.

That look had crossed her mind more times than she cared to recall.

As did the riddle of why he was so against regaining his freedom.

He hadn't needed to marry her. This wasn't the Middle Ages, where marriage was paramount in ensuring one's child's legitimacy. He didn't love her, granted. But he hadn't had to marry her. *But he had*.

The Emiliano she knew wasn't that selfless when it came to his freedom. Hadn't she, in the months before their relationship had started, predicted when his liaisons would end with almost clockwork precision? And hadn't that end been triggered by the first signs of clinginess?

'I'm here for you both,' he'd said. At the time, pain had been the dominant force riding her. Now, with time and distance, she thought, might she have dismissed those words too hastily? When they'd *both* agreed that their marriage primarily benefitted their child?

On the day she'd left Argentina, she'd breached the cold silence between them to let him know she wouldn't stand in the way of maintaining equal custody of their child. He'd coldly replied that they wouldn't need to discuss custody if they stayed married.

She shook her head now, feeling a little pathetic for desperately trying to find a salve for the constant wildfire that was her pain. A fire she feared she would never be able to put out.

Grabbing her laptop, she settled on the sofa and brought up the list of properties she'd put together for a possible viewing. Having made a shortlist, she was about to make an appointment when her phone rang.

David Hunter.

She'd sent him an email thanking him for his concern after having come home to dozens of messages from him. She'd declined his further calls about finding her a job. She was financially sound enough for now not to need a job right away. Although that would soon need to change.

She eyed the ringing phone then picked it up at the last moment.

'David, hello.'

'Sienna! Good to hear your voice,' he responded eagerly then checked himself. 'Um, I mean, I thought I would be talking to your voicemail again,' he semijoked.

'What can I do for you?' Her gaze landed on the sidebar of the property website and took note of the giddy advertisement for love and happiness, and her heart lurched.

Today was Valentine's Day. Hopelessly commercialised, but a day for lovers the world over nonetheless.

The day Emiliano would've married someone else…

But he hadn't.

Because he married you!

She pushed the insistent voice away as David cleared his throat. 'Uh, I know you aren't looking for anything right now, but I think I have something that might interest you.'

'Why?'

'It's a start-up, but the CEO thinks you might be able to put your own stamp on the job. And it's completely flexible. Hell, you can work from home if you want.'

She frowned. 'It sounds a little too good to be true. No start-up hedge fund can offer terms like that unless they're prepared to make a huge initial loss.'

'Well, this guy is pretty confident he can make things work. But he insists he wants you. And the meeting has to be today. He's flying out of the country tomorrow.'

Sienna looked down at herself and grimaced. She'd taken a shower this morning but she'd slipped back into her comfy onesie, preparing for a day of mindless TV to drown her pain.

She opened her mouth to say no then reconsidered. Her funds wouldn't last for ever, and if this offer was real she owed it to herself to consider it.

'Okay, where do I need to go?'

'It's just out of the city. He'll send a car for you. In, say, half an hour?'

'Uh…okay.'

'Great. Good luck, Sienna.' The wish was deep and heartfelt.

Frowning a little, she said goodbye and hung up.

Rising, she went to her small bedroom and critically

examined her wardrobe. She hadn't been in the mood for clothes shopping since her return, and with her expanding waistline most of her clothes no longer fit. Her gaze lit on a cashmere batwing-style jumper dress Emiliano had bought for her on a visit to Milan. The memories they evoked threatened to clog her throat but she had no time for painful trips down memory lane.

Briskly she tugged it off the hanger and slipped it on. The grey-and-black colourblock design was professional enough to pass muster. Adding tights and a pair of soft grey heeled boots, she caught her hair up in a loose but stylish bun. She was shrugging into her coat when her doorbell sounded.

Grabbing her handbag, she shut her front door. The February wind threatened to chill her to the bone as she hurried. The sight of the idling limo gave her momentary pause, but she wasn't unaccustomed to CEOs in her field of work wooing fund managers this way. Nodding to the driver, she settled into the back seat. An hour later, they turned into a long driveway.

The country house in Surrey was a stunning Georgian masterpiece. Sienna fell in love with it long before the limo pulled up to the imposing double front doors.

Stepping out, she walked up the shallow steps and pressed the bell.

For a moment, when he opened the door, she couldn't believe her eyes. Didn't want to. And then she didn't want to blink in case he was a figment of her imagination.

When he exhaled and swung the door wider, she took a short, desperate breath.

'Is this some sort of joke, Emiliano?'

'No, *amante*. This is far from a joke.' His voice was deep. Solemn. His eyes pleading.

She swung her head towards the limo. The *departing* limo.

'Come in, Sienna. *Por favor.*'

It was either stand out in the freezing cold or step into the warmth. Her feet moved forward before she'd given them complete control.

When the door shut behind her, she turned. For a moment, she couldn't find her voice. Emiliano dressed all in black had always had that power over her. This time wasn't any different. She didn't want to acknowledge the way the black sweater moulded his muscular chest or the tailored trousers clung to his powerful thighs.

So she dragged her gaze up to his.

'What is the meaning of this?'

'Give me ten minutes of your time. After that, if you want to leave I will send for the driver.'

Ten minutes. Not much time, considering the wasteland of pain that stretched before her. And this unexpected chance to be in his electrifying presence again, breathe him in, felt too hard to refuse.

Again her body reacted without total consent from her mind, her nod triggering a similar nod from him.

He led the way down a light oak-panelled hallway into a study. To one side, floor-to-ceiling bookshelves held hundreds of books. On the other side, a teak desk held pride of place. It was there that Emiliano headed. But he didn't take a seat. Instead, he reached across the desk and picked up a single sheet of paper.

'My next venture is one I intend to pour my heart and soul into, so I have taken a leaf out of your book and made a list.'

She gasped, her breath clogging in her chest. 'Emiliano...'

Turbulent eyes stopped her. 'Hear me out, Sienna. Please.'

She gestured for him to continue.

'For this venture, I need a partner who will steer me true. Who will forgive me when I misstep—and I will occasionally, because I'm not perfect. I need a partner whose trust I hope to gain and who knows she can rely on me day or night. I need a queen who will bear my children, love them and me without reserve, even when we mess up. I need a partner who will hold my heart in her hands the way I hope she will let me hold hers. I need a partner who will believe me when I say I will *always*, without exception, put her first.'

He lowered his hand, holding her captive with his mesmerising gaze.

'*Por favor, querida*, I need *you*.'

'Oh... Emiliano.'

He shuddered hard, emotion exploding from his eyes as the paper dropped from his fingers and floated to the floor, forgotten. In one desperate lunge, he arrived in front of her. 'I need you, Sienna. I *love* you. You think I married you because of our child. I married you because I couldn't see a day in my future that you weren't a part of. And, yes, I was terrified that if you knew *how* your accident happened you would leave me. If I hadn't dragged you out into that alley that night, you wouldn't have fallen. But, believe me, I would've come for you, fought tooth and nail for you. I only found out the day before you returned from South America where you'd gone. My pilots were on standby to fly out to Peru the next morning.' He shook his head. 'Seeing you in that restaurant with Hunter made me lose my mind.'

'Seeing you on that magazine cover with Graciela made me lose mine,' she confessed huskily.

'*Lo siento*. If it's any consolation, know that I've never messed up anything in my life the way I messed up then. And I will move mountains to make sure I don't cause you pain like that ever again.'

The solid promise in his words made her heart stutter, then beat wildly against her ribs. 'I love you. I was going to tell you that night…on my birthday. I was going to be brave and put my feelings out there,' she confessed brokenly. 'Tell you about my past, tell you I didn't care who knew about us, ask if you would be mine the way I was yours.'

He squeezed his eyes shut and his chest heaved in an audible inhale. '*Dios mío*. Forgive me, *mi corazón*. I beg you.'

'Tell me you love me again. Please. I would feel so much better.'

'I love you. *Te amo*. I love your bravery, your spirit, your kind heart. I love your body. I love your soul.' His hand dropped to her gently swollen belly. 'I love that our baby is nestled warm and safe inside your body. I love—'

She flung herself at him, shameless, happy tears spilling from her eyes as she pressed her mouth against his.

With a helpless groan, he caught her up against him, deepening the kiss almost immediately. Claiming her.

An eternity later, he lifted his head, brushed away her tears. 'The past few weeks have been hell, *querida*,' he muttered. 'Enough for me to confess I don't even mind these tears this time, because seeing them means you're here in front of me, not a figment of my desperate imagination.'

She laughed. Kissed him again just because she could. Of course that led to heat being generated at an alarming rate. Which led to her being scooped up in strong arms, carried to the living room, undressed and laid on a sheepskin rug before the roaring fire.

It led to exquisite lovemaking that had her crying out in ecstasy and wonder. And, afterwards, softly murmured admissions of love in dual tongues.

'I can't believe you used David,' she mused many hours later.

Her husband shrugged arrogantly. Oh, how she'd missed that shrug.

'He needed to be made aware that you were off limits

to him in this lifetime and the next. I merely utilised his expertise, and he earned a fat commission in the bargain. Win-win.'

She laughed. He joined in. Then they both sobered and stared deep into each other's eyes, letting their feelings speak for a moment.

'I asked myself how I could fall in love with you twice in one lifetime,' she whispered, her thumb tracing his full lower lip.

His fingers traced reverentially along her jaw. 'And?' he demanded gruffly.

'It was because my heart knew you were the one. My heart will always know you and love you, *mi amor*.'

'As will mine.'

EPILOGUE

'OKAY, *MI ÁNGEL*. Time for our big moment in the spotlight. I'll try and keep it together if you will. Deal?'

Emiliano smiled as he entered the nursery to the sight of his brother cradling his eight-week-old daughter. The size disparity was ridiculous, as was the extracautious way Matias was cradling Angelina, but his heart flipped over all the same.

He was getting used to that feeling. Getting used to it knocking him for six several dozen times a day. It started from the moment he woke up next to the woman of his heart, the woman who made him glad to be alive every day. Then it went on, a relentless insanity he never wanted to be cured of.

'You know she can't high-five you just yet, right, *mi hermano*? Or even understand a word you're saying?'

Matias spun carefully on his heel, his gaze touching briefly on Emiliano before returning to the treasure in his arms. 'Of course she can. I'm her godfather, which means we share a special bond. She smiled and pumped her fist just before you interrupted us.'

Shaking his head, Emiliano strolled closer, the magic of his daughter impossible to resist. He caressed her soft cheek with the back of his finger, his heart expanding when she leaned into him.

Angelina's eyes, a soft turquoise at birth, were slowly changing, taking on her mother's green eyes. Her hair was also soot-black like Sienna's, and Emiliano secretly hoped his daughter would take every single one of her mother's attributes, both inside and out. Every element of his wife's character and spirit deserved celebration.

'You look like a sap, you know that?' Matias mocked. But Emiliano noted the gruffness in his voice.

'What can I say? I'm a lucky man and I'm not ashamed to show it.'

'*Sí*, you are indeed lucky. As I am, after what you did.' The gaze that met his was solemn and fiercely sincere. It also held a brotherhood that Emiliano had severely missed and almost lost. 'I know what you risked for me. You have my undying gratitude.'

'You would've done the same for me.' He knew that in his soul and was only beginning to appreciate what that truly meant. He clasped his brother on the shoulder and deep understanding passed between them.

His daughter gurgled and his attention was immediately absorbed by her once more. Leaning down, he inhaled her sweet baby scent before kissing her gently on the forehead.

'Yeah, I still think you need to dial down the mush, though. It's unbecoming in a grown man,' Matias chided.

'Says the man who wept when I asked him to be godfather.'

Matias snorted. 'You shouted the question at me when I was in the middle of training a temperamental filly and I got kicked for my troubles. I invite you to experience that and tell me whether you wouldn't shed a tear, too.'

Emiliano laughed. After a few seconds Matias joined in. They were still laughing when his wife, the reason for his heartbeat, walked in.

'There you are. I was beginning to think you three had hopped on a plane and hightailed it for Tahiti.'

Sienna tried not stumble as two sets of tawny eyes looked up from her daughter and met hers across the nursery. One set held an everlasting love she still pinched herself over each time she felt that visceral connection. The other held warmth, acceptance and love.

Matias had made a full recovery since waking up from

his coma eight months ago. After having been released from the private Swiss hospital, he'd moved into the Cordoba mansion with them, Emiliano having decided to split his work life between Argentina and London.

Once Matias had completely recovered, he'd resumed the reins of Castillo Estate on the proviso that Benito and Valentina retired and relinquished all say in the running of the estate to him. They'd agreed and had since embarked on a world cruise, courtesy of Emiliano's yacht. Emiliano had deemed it a small price to pay to be rid of them for a while.

The relationship between Benito and Emiliano had altered for the better since the night Sienna had regained her memory. She held out hope for a further thawing in Valentina's character, as well. But, for now, she had all the family she needed.

A family she worshipped with every fibre of her being.

Emiliano held out his arm and she swayed to his side, accepting his kiss before smiling down at her precious daughter.

'The guests are waiting. This little angel needs to make her christening debut.'

The christening attendees included new friends they'd made here in Argentina and old acquaintances turned friends from London. The intimate affair was just what they'd both wanted.

'Let them wait a while longer. She is a female and it's her day. I believe it's her divine right to be fashionably late,' Emiliano said.

When Angelina gurgled her agreement, they all laughed. While Matias smiled with complete infatuation at his niece, Sienna's eyes met her husband's.

'*Te amo, mi corazón,*' he whispered against her lips. '*Para siempre.*'

* * * * *

If you enjoyed
THE BOSS'S NINE-MONTH NEGOTIATION,
take a look at these other
ONE NIGHT WITH CONSEQUENCES
themed stories!

CLAIMING HIS CHRISTMAS CONSEQUENCE
by Michelle Smart
THE GUARDIAN'S VIRGIN WARD
by Caitlin Crews
A CHILD CLAIMED BY GOLD
by Rachael Thomas
THE CONSEQUENCE OF HIS VENGEANCE
by Jennie Lucas
SECRETS OF A BILLIONAIRE'S MISTRESS
by Sharon Kendrick

Available now!

MILLS & BOON®

MODERN™

POWER, PASSION AND IRRESISTIBLE TEMPTATION

A sneak peek at next month's titles...

In stores from 6th April 2017:

- **The Sheikh's Bought Wife** – Sharon Kendrick
- **The Magnate's Tempestuous Marriage** – Miranda Lee
- **Bound by the Sultan's Baby** – Carol Marinelli
- **Di Marcello's Secret Son** – Rachael Thomas

In stores from 4th May 2017:

- **The Innocent's Shameful Secret** – Sara Craven
- **The Forced Bride of Alazar** – Kate Hewitt
- **Blackmailed Down the Aisle** – Louise Fuller
- **The Italian's Vengeful Seduction** – Bella Frances

MILLS & BOON®

EXCLUSIVE EXTRACT

Persuading plain Jane to marry him was easy
enough – but Shiekh Zayed Al Zawba hadn't
bargained on the irresistible curves hidden under
her clothes, or that she is deliciously untouched.
When Jane begins to tempt him beyond his
wildest dreams, leaving their marriage
unconsummated becomes impossible…

Read on for a sneak preview of
THE SHEIKH'S BOUGHT WIFE

It was difficult to be *distant* when your body seemed to
have developed a stubborn will of its own. When she found
herself wanting to push her aching breasts against Zayed's
powerful chest as he caught her in his arms for the traditional first dance between bride and groom. As it was, she
could barely think straight and wasn't it the most infuriating
thing in the world that he immediately seemed to pick up
on that?

'You seem to be having trouble breathing, dear wife,'
he murmured as he moved her to the center of the marble
dance floor.

'The dress is very tight.'

'I'd noticed.' He twirled her around, holding her back
a little. 'It looks very well on you.'

She forced a tight smile but she didn't relax. 'Thank you.'

'Or maybe it is the excitement of having me this close
to you which is making you pant like a little kitten?'

'You're *annoying* me, rather than exciting me. And I do
wish you'd stop trying to get underneath my skin.'

'Don't you like people getting underneath your skin, Jane?'

'No,' she said honestly. 'I don't.'

'Why not?'

She met the blaze of his ebony eyes and suppressed a shiver. 'Does everything have to have a reason?'

'In my experience, yes.' There was a pause. 'Has a man hurt you in the past?'

This was her chance to tell him yes—even though the very idea that someone had got that close to her was laughable.

Zayed had already guessed she might be a virgin, but that didn't even come close to her shameful lack of experience.

Trying to ignore the way his groin was brushing against her as he edged her closer, she glanced up at him, her cheeks burning. 'I refuse to answer that on the grounds that I might incriminate myself. Tell me instead, do you always insist on interrogating women when you're dancing with them?'

'No. I don't,' he said simply. 'But then I've never had a bride before and I've never danced with a woman who was so determined not to give anything of herself away.'

'And that's the only reason you want to know,' she said quietly. 'Because you like a challenge.'

'All men like a challenge, Jane.' His black eyes gleamed. 'Haven't you learned that by now?'

She didn't answer—because how was she qualified to answer any questions about what men did or didn't like?

Don't miss
THE SHEIKH'S BOUGHT WIFE
By Sharon Kendrick

Available May 2017
www.millsandboon.co.uk

Join Britain's BIGGEST Romance Book Club

- **EXCLUSIVE offers every month**
- **FREE delivery direct to your door**
- **NEVER MISS a title**
- **EARN Bonus Book points**

Call Customer Services
0844 844 1358*

or visit
millsandboon.co.uk/subscriptions

* This call will cost you 7 pence per minute plus your phone company's price per minute access charge.

CB3